PRINCE CHARMING

K WEBSTER

CHAPTER ONE

WINSTON

FLASH. FLASH. FLASH.

I'm posing like a goddamn Versace model to please my insufferable mother when I'd rather be playing naughty games with *her*.

My assistant.

My worthless maid.

My obedient, dirty girl who gets off on the same depraved shit I do.

Soon enough.

I just have to make it through this bullshit first.

Tilt your head a little to the right. No, a bit more to the left. Angle down slightly. Stare intently into the camera. Do the serious scowl thing again. Now switch it up and give us a smirk.

This is more Perry's scene. Strutting around like a rooster so everyone will admire him. It's a waste of my time to preen in front of a camera when I could be doing something more productive. One cursory glance of the courtyard tells me either he's late or choosing to avoid this shitshow. I'll gripe his ass out later for bailing on me.

Smile, Mr. Constantine. I said smile, not grimace. Are you ill, sir?

This goes on for eons. Mother takes great pleasure in my displeasure based on the sly grin curving up one side of her lips. It's times like these, despite me being a grown-ass man, I wish my father were here to intervene. He was always the warmer of our two parents and seemed to be one of the few who could thaw her out. After the first half hour of indulging Mother with photographs, he'd have pulled me aside for "business." We'd have hidden out until the party started, cracking open a sixty-five-thousand-dollar bottle of Louis XIII Black Pearl Cognac as we enjoyed a few moments of silent bliss.

The bitterness of losing my father rears its ugly head. My spine goes rigid, and my scowl deepens.

That's the look. Right there. Money shot, sir. Perhaps narrow your eyes a bit. Show them you mean business.

My phone buzzes in my pocket. I itch to pull it out and take the call. The pictures Ash sent me of her all dolled up in the gown were breathtaking. It makes me crave to dirty her up and ruin her. I'd been about to tell her that too when I was dragged back to the photoshoot where I've been miserable ever since. Knowing my spoiled girl was expecting "endless amounts of praise" when I haven't had an opportunity to shower her with it yet or even send money for the photos sits in the pit of my stomach like a lead balloon. If it weren't for my need to put on a good show for the public, I'd have shut this circus down already. I didn't exponentially grow my father's company since his death by being stubborn or obtuse. No, I did it because I know the necessary games that must be played. Agreeing to a magazine spread that showcases the power the Constantine name possesses with my smiling face and expensive suit on the cover is just one of those moves that must be made in order to stay on top. Sometimes the ones beneath me need a reminder of the force behind the dominating name.

When the photographer stops to look at the settings on his camera, I pull my phone from my pocket. I have a missed text from her and one from Perry.

> **Ash:** Winston, I'm sorry lover, but I won't be able to make it to the party. While it was lovely using you for your money, I won't need it

anymore. My brothers will look after me now.

I reread the text three more times.

It's not her. My gut tells me it's not.

And even though I haven't rewarded her yet like she craves, she wouldn't jump to such a harsh reply.

The girl is practically in love. I finally gave her the fucking she's been begging for and spent the night with her. It means one of those little triplet shits thought it'd be funny to pretend to be her. Irritation spreads across my flesh like a fever, scalding and dizzying me. If I hadn't invited the entire Mannford clan to the birthday ball, I'd be a little worried about her being with them. But, since Dr. Mannford is almost as reliable as my mother when it comes to social appearances, I shelve my concern for now because everyone will be here soon. I'll refrain from texting her back in case one of those dickheads took her phone. I read Perry's text next.

> **Perry:** *Something came up. I had to run out, but I'll return shortly. I always got your back, Winny.*

His words strike me as odd, but I also find a sense of relief in them.

"Sir, could you put your phone away? We still

have a few more shots," the photographer calls out in an exasperated tone, distracting me from Perry.

"I'm sorry," I rumble, piercing the man with a hard stare. "For a second there, I thought *I* was Winston Constantine who owned this entire goddamn city."

He recoils at my harsh words. "I only meant—"

"That's enough, darling," Mother purrs as she sashays over to us, dismissing the photographer with an annoyed flick of her wrist that's weighed down with sparkly jewels. "You've taken enough photos."

The photographer nods and then proceeds to pack up with his head bowed. Mother takes my elbow and points to a pathway covered with an ornate carpet meant for walking on during the party so as not to destroy the grass. Once we're safely on the carpet, we stroll toward the estate at a leisurely pace. The guests will be arriving any moment now, but they'll be taking photographs out front and then ushered into the piano room where they'll enjoy some music from a young recent Julliard grad concert pianist, hors d'oeuvres, and champagne until it's time for dinner. We still have time before the event starts.

"You're awfully surly this afternoon," Mother

says casually, though I don't miss the accusatory tone. "Something on your mind?"

Someone.

But I sure as fuck am not telling her that.

"Work is keeping me busy," I grunt out instead.

She lets out a heavy sigh. "Your work ethic is that of your father's, bordering on obsessive. Do you ever pause to enjoy the fruit of your labor, love?"

The forbidden fruit.

Why, yes, Mother.

"On occasion." I smirk at her. "I'm nearly forty, not fourteen. Why the sudden concern?"

"A mother can't be worried about her little boy?"

The sarcasm in her tone makes my lips twitch with amusement. "Not the one I grew up with. What is it you're really vexed about?"

"It's Perry."

We stop, and I lift a brow at her. Her face has been beautifully made up today, making her seem as young as one of my sisters. It's a shame she'll never know love again. Despite her icy façade most times, I know it broke her heart when Dad died five years ago. The kind of break you never really heal from.

It's one of the things I loathe about coming here.

The memories. The feelings. The pain.

While the Constantine compound isn't your typical home, it was mine. I grew up loved and adored by my parents, especially my father. As they added children to the fray, and I just became the eldest in a pecking order, I learned to harden myself to certain feelings. Perry still has much to learn as he's the Constantine who wears his emotions like a big, blinking neon sign for everyone to see. Even Keaton, the baby boy in our family, has taken a page from Mother's book and can keep his shit in check.

"He's actually doing great," I admit. "Don't tell him I said it."

She laughs, rich and warm and real. "Oh, Son, not about work. I swear it's all you think about."

Though she likes to play coy, Mother is pleased I flawlessly took the reins when Dad died. I'm the only one capable of holding the leash to the living, breathing, snarling mega-beast that is our nearly limitless fortune.

"Keeping this empire going is a full-time job." I cut my eyes to her, not missing the brief flash of pain. We both know why I'm running this empire. Because he can't. And Mother may play her innocent games, but we all know who the real puppet master behind our family name is. She just chooses to quietly ruin people where I prefer to flaunt it like a new, tailored suit.

"It's his car." She lets out a frustrated sigh. "He's so naïve he doesn't realize he's even doing it."

"Doing what?"

"Trying my patience."

I bite back a grin. Perry isn't always the favored golden child. "Do tell, Mother. You know how much I enjoy hearing of whenever he disappoints you."

Her eyes flash with mirth. "You're awful sometimes. Just like your father."

My father was a hard man when it called for it. Being a Constantine, that was often. But he could be funny at times. He loved his children no doubt. A comparison to him is one I don't mind at all.

"I apologize," I say with a grin that absolutely says otherwise. "Continue. Let's hear what the unruly toddler did and how I can fix it."

Her severe features soften, and she plucks a non-existent hair off my lapel. The simple gesture is one my siblings never notice. Mother is cold most days and hardly affectionate, but she has her ways. Simple ones. Sure, she showers us with over-the-top gifts and praise—though some of us she prefers over others—but sometimes it's the small things. For as long as I can remember, she would smooth out the hair on our heads or pull off stray lint from our clothes or tap on our nose when it was required of us to smile. Though she doesn't fuss over our hair or touch our noses any longer, she still does the other. It's a reminder of why my father loved her. Somewhere, deep inside, she's soft for her family.

"Can you speak to him about his vehicle?"

I frown at her. "He got a new car?"

"Halcyon is paying for it," she tosses back, her lip curling into a disgusted sneer. "While I appreciate you giving him a car allowance, I wish you'd have been there to help him pick one out."

I'm amused that she's put out over a car. There's no telling what sort of monstrosity my brother chose. If we're basing it on his last car—a restored muscle car, much to Mother's horror— then whatever it is must be even more obnoxious. I'd never tell her, but I quite enjoy seeing the vein in her forehead throb whenever his Ford Mustang Shelby GT350 roars into the drive, the loud V-8 rumbling with enough power to make the windows rattle.

"His Mustang is one of the best sports cars priced under a hundred grand," I taunt, reciting my brother's words back to her. "Zero to sixty in four point two seconds."

"Don't remind me," she grumbles. "Even that, I could tolerate, because it wasn't an eye sore. His new car is hideous. Try, if you will, to have him reconsider the purchase. If it comes from me, I'll just sound like a meddling mother."

Mother never wants to disappoint the favorite child. She can be harsh, abrasive, cruel even, but when she's playing favorites, she goes all out.

"I'll see what I can do," I lie. I won't. He's a Constantine. The Constantine men in this family are serious about their cars. Even Dad had his particular desires when it came to his vehicles—which is fitting he passed away in his favorite one. I can give Perry a lot of shit about everything from his hairstyle to his clothing to his lack of business sense. What I won't do is insult his car or tell him his mommy doesn't like it.

Keaton steps outside, and I take it as my cue to untangle myself from my mother. My baby brother, who looks striking like our mother but is built like a brick shithouse, pins his wolfish smile on me. I tip my head at him and call out.

"Got a minute to talk business, little brother?"

Keaton's eyes dart to Mother before he nods. "Always a minute for you."

"Honestly, Winston," Mother complains, though there's an edge of humor in her tone. "It's your birthday. Give it a rest."

We both know she'd love for me to convince Keaton to follow in my footsteps rather than whatever grandiose ideas he has about professionally playing rugby. I feel a sliver of pity for him as I remember being his age—headed toward my last year in prep school—wishing for more out of life than what was predestined for me. But, with age, you learn family is everything, and how you continue that legacy is all that matters.

"No rest for the wicked. I'll catch up in a bit," I say, taking mother's dainty hand and kissing the top of it. "Excuse me."

"Enjoy your birthday, love," Mother calls out behind me. "Save me a dance later."

I smirk as I approach Keaton. It's a shame he's not older. I'm stuck with Perry at the office, but Keaton's the brainiac. He's got the whole asshole jock vibe going on, unfortunately like the fucking triplet twats, but unlike those dipshits, Keaton's mind is sharp and calculating. There's no doubt in my mind he'll bag the valedictorian accolade at

Pembroke his senior year.

"Thirsty?" I arch a brow at him.

"Depends. What are we drinking?"

I clutch his shoulder and squeeze. "Dad's stash."

The smugness rolling off him melts away as vulnerability flashes in his gaze. Like the rest of the Constantines, he was greatly impacted by the loss of our father, probably the most of all of us. Where Perry was an emotionally wrecked teenager, Keaton went from a playful, happy preteen to one formed of stone. Impenetrable and hard. That, I can relate to.

We step inside the estate, slipping past bustling waitstaff as they rush around in a frenzy to make the party a success. I avoid the sounds of piano playing nearby, striding down a series of hallways until I find Dad's study. It's been locked because of the guests, but I quickly unlock it with my key and grant us access. Keaton closes the door behind him as I make a beeline over to Dad's liquor cabinet that remains just the way it always has been, thanks to Mother. Each of her children have raided it, needing to feel that closeness to our father, and each time, she replaces the emptied liquor as though it were never touched.

Keaton takes a seat at one of the oversized leather armchairs while I open the mahogany cabinet. My eyes widen at the new addition. A 24-karot gold dipped with platinum bottle of Henri IV Dudognon Heritage Cognac Grande Champagne encrusted in tiny crystals with a navy-blue ribbon tied around the neck of it.

Mother.

Most mothers would buy their son a tie for his thirty-seventh birthday.

Mine surprises me with a two-million-dollar bottle of cognac.

"Looks like we're celebrating in a way Dad would approve of," I tell Keaton, holding up the bottle.

He smirks and gives me an arrogant nod of his head. "If she got you that for your birthday and she barely likes you, imagine what she'll get me."

I flip him off and then pour us each a glass. Carrying them over to him, I study my brother along the way. He has the cool, aloof demeanor that is fitting for a Constantine, but I know he burns inside. His eyes are telling, often flashing with emotion he otherwise keeps well hidden.

"I miss this," I admit as I pass off his glass and take a seat across from him.

"Hanging with the best-looking Constantine?"

"No, I see that guy in the mirror each day. Gets rather boring if we're being honest." I smirk at him. "I'm talking about Dad. This was our thing."

The muscle in his jaw ticks, and he hides it by bringing the glass to his lips, inhaling the scent, before taking a sip. "Hmph."

I nearly bark out a laugh at his childish response. Sometimes, though, I have to remind myself, he still is one. A child. In the fall, he'll head back to Vermont and finish his time at Pembroke Preparatory School. Then he'll become a real man, following in the footsteps of each male Constantine before him—aside from Perry's slacker ass—carving out a powerful name for himself. Rugby will likely become a distant dream, just as it was for me.

"He'd always tell Mother we had important matters to discuss between men," I say, my lips turning up at the fond memory. "And we'd get borderline drunk on his stash. Later, Mother would threaten us within inches of our lives if we embarrassed her."

Five years.

It's been five long years since I had those moments with my father that I selfishly took for granted.

"Are we ever going to discuss the elephant in the room?" he demands in a moody tone that's more fitting for Perry.

My brow hikes up. "The fact your girlfriend isn't with you?"

"She'll be here later." His eyes pull from mine like they did when he was a child and hiding something. "I'm talking about what's eating you. You're all worked up. We don't do heart to hearts, Win, so spill."

I study him for a beat, impressed with his ability to sniff out my weakness, which is difficult for most men, never mind a teenager. "How close are you with the Mannford triplets?"

After some research, I discovered Dr. Mannford got them into Pembroke the second semester of their junior year.

"The new kids?" Keaton takes another drink and shrugs. "They stay on their turf, and I stay on mine. They don't fuck with me."

"You're not a gangster, Keat. Explain this in civilized adult terms."

He rolls his eyes, reminding me of his age again. "I mean, I don't talk to them if I don't have to. Pembroke is less about social standing and more about circles. My circle is rugby and theirs is lacrosse. Those circles don't often overlap. And they aren't welcome in the Hellfire Club."

I almost snort. Just the mention of the Pembroke Club that ruled all others brings back memories of prep school dustups. But I have to focus on the now. "Your circles don't often overlap, but sometimes they do?"

"It's like this. We're lions. They're the hyenas feeding off our scraps. There's no partnership, only awareness." Leaning forward, he sets down his glass on the table between us. "Why the sudden interest in the Mannfords?"

"They're…" I trail off and scratch at my jaw as I ponder how to word this without it getting back to Mother. "They're overstepping into *my circle*. They're on *my turf*. I want to know how this affects you if I kick them out of play."

His blue eyes flash with interest. "It would entertain me greatly."

"Something we both can agree on." I sip my drink, my attention lasered on my little brother. "Could you do me a favor?"

"Favors will cost you."

I bark out a laugh, because I love this kid. Fucking Constantine through and through.

"Naturally," I rumble. "Name your price."

Our negotiation has my thoughts drifting

back to Ash and her mysterious text. Something I will get to the bottom of soon enough.

"It all depends on the favor." He shrugs, but his eyes are shrewd, clearly invested in our negotiation. "Let's hear it."

"For now, I only want information. Not the bullshit Ulrich can get either. That's common knowledge."

Ulrich, our family's most trusted private investigator, is the one who helped Mother uncover what she did on my ex, Meredith, and information on Dad's "accident" that has every single fucking Constantine questioning his death.

"What then?" Keaton probes. "Like who they're fucking?"

"Again, common knowledge. I imagine anything with a skirt." I twirl the liquid around in my glass, enjoying the heady scent of it. "I want to know what makes them tick. I need to know how to detonate them with one push of a button."

His brow lifts, amusement contorting his handsome features. "You're such a dick sometimes."

We both laugh, because he's one too.

"Fine," he says after a moment. "I'll get you your information."

"And what do you get, baby Keat?"

He stands and walks over to the liquor cabinet, picking up the bottle we've been drinking from. "This. Your birthday gift."

"Little shit," I grumble over my shoulder. "Fine. It's a deal."

I don't tell him my real birthday gift will be when Cinderelliott gets on her knees and chokes on my cock. Because, if he knew, he'd want that instead, especially once he realizes Ash is his age. He might convince Mother he's in love with the prissy little rich girl he's with, but I know better. She's nothing more than a tool to be used in his agenda, whatever that may be. Another reason to add to the list of why my family can't know about this girl.

Each and every one of them will try and take her from me in some way.

Except Perry.

For the first time in… ever… the golden child is my favorite, too.

CHAPTER TWO

ASH

I CAN DO this.

I'm not some run-of-the-mill damsel in distress.

Women who can go toe-to-toe with a Constantine and hold their own don't faint at the first sign of danger. And though I'm shaking like a leaf with tears steadily streaming down my cheeks, I won't let this assault stop me.

I'll make it to that birthday ball, find my dark prince, and show those twisted triplets they've messed with the wrong girl. They may scare the hell out of me, but my inner fire begs to be unleashed so I can watch them burn.

My mind races with rampant thoughts. Most of them revenge filled. Some of them terrified and cowed, especially when I think of Leo and the rest of the Morellis. But the thoughts that keep me powering forward are of *him*.

Winston Constantine.

My fucked-up Prince Charming.

The games we play are ours, and I won't let those psycho stepbrothers of mine or Leo Morelli make me feel ashamed of them. Win gets me in a way no one else does. But, though I'm not embarrassed of what goes on between us, and I'm certain neither is he, I can't discount the fact that there are ripple effects that could ultimately harm us in the end. That's why I can't be cavalier and assume he's going to rescue me from this situation.

No, I have to think like Winston.

There's a way to get the triplets back. I'm sure I'll find it, too. They see me as this weak girl they can toy with and control. They're playing with fire even though they don't realize it yet.

As for Morelli…

That's going to take a little more thought.

Winston can help me with Scout and his scary shadows, but Leo was pretty clear about his threats. I'll figure something out. Once I've rested and had time to think.

Right now, I have a party to get ready for.

The doorbell rings, and I startle. I swipe the rest of my smeared makeup off my face before tossing the washcloth back into the sink. The bell rings again. By the time I reach the door, I'm out of breath. Standing on the other side is Perry Constantine, ravishing in a tuxedo.

His concerned expression transforms into one of fury. All plans to be brave and vengeful fly out the window in this moment. I burst into tears, thankful to have someone on my side after the horrible crap I just endured.

"Fuck, Ash," Perry growls, pulling me to him in a fierce hug. "What the hell happened to you?"

He squeezes me tight, holding all the cracked and brittle pieces of me together. I allow myself a few ragged sobs before I'm reeling it back. Sniffling and swallowing down the emotion. There's no time for this. I pull from his embrace, swiping at my eyes with the palms of my hands.

"Long story," I croak out. "Right now, I need your help."

Turning on my heel, I rush up the stairs to grab my bag. His heavy footfalls behind me are comforting. As soon as we enter my room, he lets out a string of curse words.

"What the fuck happened?" he demands, gesturing at my ruined dress on the floor. "Don't give me the 'long story' bullshit. Your brothers did this to you?"

"Step," I hiss, shoving the contents of my backpack they'd yanked out earlier back inside and zipping it. "They're assholes."

Perry shakes his head, blue eyes flashing with anger. "This is beyond asshole behavior. This is insanity. It's assault." His face pales. "Wait… Did they…"

"No," I rush out, swiping at another tear. "Just cut my dress up and did their best to ruin me."

He scowls and lifts a thumb to my lip, brushing over the cut Scout gave me when he kissed me. "They hurt you."

"Scout did that, but don't worry, it's the worst of it."

His eyes penetrate me as he attempts to read past the surface. Of course there's more to it. He may be the nice Constantine, but he's still a Constantine—able to smell bullshit from a mile away. But, unlike Winston, he doesn't demand answers or do everything in his power to extract them. It's better that Perry came to my rescue rather than Winston. There's no telling what Winston would do if he saw me in a wrecked state he had no part in.

Why?

Because he cares.

Right?

My self-doubt wars with logic.

As much as he would like to deny it, I know deep down he does. We wouldn't have gotten ourselves in this mess to begin with if he didn't. But I often wonder if it's enough. Could someone like Winston Constantine—intense, handsome, incredibly successful—tie himself to a woman of not only another class entirely, but someone half his age? I'd like to think we have more in common than what appears on the surface. Only time will tell, I guess. Time. How much do we have? I push away the nagging memory of his words, of how I'm only his entertainment for this year, and next year it'll be a yacht or a car.

"You can't go to the party looking like that," Perry utters, frustration evident in his tone. "You know that, right?" He sighs and pulls out his phone, sending a tremor of apprehension skittering through me. "Hold on. I know what to do."

"Who are you calling?"

"Reinforcements."

He starts talking on the phone, barking out orders in a way that reminds me of his older brother. I follow him out of the room and down the stairs. Once outside, my eyebrows lift at his car. He ends the call, pocketing the phone and chuckling.

"Sweet ride, am I right?"

I try not to grimace. "It's so… orange."

"It's a 1969 Chevy Chevelle. Custom exterior and interior. Seventeen-inch wheels. A 454 big-block engine." He flashes me a boyish grin. "Total chick magnet."

That smile of his is the chick magnet, not the bright orange beast of a car.

"It looks like a pumpkin," I blurt out, laughing.

"A pumpkin with badass white racing stripes and white leather interior." He flips me off as he opens the passenger side door. "Your carriage to the ball, princess. Get in or walk. Your choice."

I pretend to consider his ultimatum, tapping my chin with my finger. "Kidding." Quickly, I hug him again. "Thank you."

"You're my brother's girl. There's nothing to thank me for."

His brother's girl.

A girl can certainly wish.

I'M STUNNED SPEECHLESS as we make our way up the driveway to what Perry calls "the Constantine compound." It's bigger than any mansion I've ever seen. Maybe a few mansions shoved together.

People are milling about everywhere, dressed in fancy gowns and tuxedos, reminding me that I have to get my ass into gear and quickly.

"I'm going to park in the garage. We'll sneak in that way," Perry assures me, flashing me a comforting smile.

I swipe my sweaty palms over the denim of my jeans. I'm thankful for Perry. There's no way I could consider doing this without his help. If I'm Cinderelliott, then Perry is most definitely my fairy godmother, which means this story is completely, irretrievably fucked up.

Perry pulls into a garage bay, the loud engine echoing against the walls and rattling my bones. After he kills the engine, we climb out, rushing into the stately home. Rather than heading toward the sounds of piano and voices, Perry ushers me down a series of hallways. I'm practically running to keep up with him.

"This way is Tinsley's room," he says, grabbing my wrist.

"Tinsley?"

"Little sister." He flashes me a grin over his shoulder. "Reinforcements."

My heart does a little flutter that Winston's siblings are helping me. I've felt so alone ever since Dad started dating Manda and then more so after they were married. I'd been delusional to be excited, at first, to have three stepbrothers. Being an only child, I always craved having siblings. Seeing how the Constantines stick together, it warms my heart, especially now that I feel like I'm a part of it.

"In here," he says, pushing into a bedroom that's bigger than the entire first floor of our brownstone. "Ash, meet Tinsley. Tins, meet Winston's…"

"Assistant," I throw out. "I'm his personal assistant. Ash Elliott."

Tinsley, dressed in white denim shorts and a pale yellow halter top, turns to look my way. Her bright blue eyes are curious, though a bit apprehensive. All the Constantine kids look alike. Perfect, golden-haired, beautiful people who could easily be models or celebrities. Tinsley, though she seems younger than Perry and me, is every bit as gorgeous as the rest of them.

"Personal assistant?" Tinsley's lips curl into an amused grin. "Is that what Winny's calling her?"

Perry chuckles. "For now. Do you have something she could wear?"

"Don't you think we ought to do something about her face and hair first?" Tinsley asks, frowning. "Mother will lose her mind if Winston's 'personal assistant' shows up looking anything less than perfect."

"Jac and Gus will be here soon. I already texted Keaton to grab them and bring them back here." Perry gestures at his little sister. "Why aren't you dressed?"

She shrugs, her bottom lip pouting out slightly. "I don't feel like it."

"Mother won't stand for a no-show, Tins," Perry says, his voice firm. "You need to get dressed."

She's saved from further big brother bossiness when the bedroom door opens, drawing all of our attention. Another Constantine, much younger than Winston but still a hot replica of him, strides in, arrogance rippling from him. His tuxedo fits him well, showcasing a muscular, athletic body. Where Tinsley and Perry have a warmness about them, something feels much colder with the new arrival.

"Keaton," Perry greets. "Where are Jac and Gus?"

"Unloading their car." Keaton's eyes land on me, and he narrows them. "You must be the charity case."

Tinsley mutters something under her breath about him being rude, and Perry clenches his jaw.

I, however, am not unnerved. If anything, he reminds me the most of Winston. And there's a familiarity in his coldness that I immediately warm to.

"In the flesh," I say with a shrug. "Winston wants me at his party. Someone thought I shouldn't go and tried to stop me. But we all know Winston gets what he wants no matter the cost."

Keaton smirks, and Perry rolls his eyes while Tinsley smothers a grin.

"We're here!" a high-pitched voice sings. "Miss Tinsley, you look ravishing. Give us fifteen minutes and you'll be ready for the—oh, sweet baby Jesus do not tell me this is what we're working our magic on!"

A small, short man with pink hair and a lip ring is gaping at me like I'm a disease he might catch. Right behind him, a heavier-set guy loaded down with bags grunts, also unsure as he sizes me up. Unlike his prissy other half, he's dressed in a T-shirt and jeans with jet-black hair styled messily on his head.

"Gustavo," the little man whines, waving a wild hand at me. "Feast your eyes on this monstrosity! This is going to be impossible. I mean, just look at all that splotchiness on her face!

Don't even get me started on the fright that's her hair!"

Keaton laughs, smacking Perry on the back. "Maybe you should be paying them double. He's right. She's a mess, man."

Perry straightens and stalks over to me. "Charge me whatever it takes, Jac, but make it happen. She needs to not only be party ready, but she needs to be the highlight of tonight. Make her stand out."

Jac scoffs. "Don't insult me. You know my brother and I are the best." He then turns to regard me with narrowed eyes, gesturing at my messy, damp bun. "The hair is going to be the most difficult part. You have a ton of it, and it's still wet. Luckily, I brought the emergency hair."

"What the fuck is emergency hair?" Keaton asks, his features more boyish now that they're contorted into a horrified expression.

"Wigs, dumbass," Perry says, shaking his head. "Come on, Keat, let's have a chat while they work on the girls."

"I'm not going," Tinsley says, straightening her spine, her voice soft but unwavering. "Please don't make me go."

The three siblings seem to converse without words, each of them eyeing each other up as though they can see into the other's head.

"She can wear my dress, not borrow one." Tinsley's blue eyes brighten as if she's sold herself on the idea and now needs to convince her brothers. "Jac brought emergency hair because he thought he was getting me ready which means Ash here can pass as a blonde."

Keaton scowls, and Perry shakes his head.

"Yes," Tinsley says, her voice a litter firmer. "No one will notice. Ash can avoid Mother, and she'll think I was there as long as Ash keeps her distance."

"Nope," Perry grunts. "Mom already texted to let us know we're expected to make toasts at midnight. You have to be there."

Tinsley deflates, her bottom lip poking out in a cute way. "Oh."

"Maybe there's a way." Keaton edges over to her, his overprotectiveness rippling in waves as he slings a muscular arm over his sister's dainty shoulders. "Ash could always attend the party, avoid Mother, and before the stroke of midnight, the two of you could swap the dress out just in time for the toasts."

A hopeful smile graces Tinsley's lips.

"That could work," I offer, wanting to help give this poor socialite the night off since it's clearly weighing heavily on her. "At a quarter till, I could meet you back here."

Perry's brows furrow as he considers our plan. "It'll just make people talk. The two of you look nothing alike."

"The only one we have to convince is Mother," Keaton argues. "Who cares about the rest? They talk anyway. Hell, it's all they ever do. Let them talk and give Tins a break."

Perry's gaze flits over his little sister before he lets out a heavy sigh. "Fine, but if you guys fuck this up, Mother is going to be livid."

I cringe as I worry about displeasing their mother.

"We won't fuck it up," I assure Perry. "I promise."

"Jac, Gus," Perry barks out. "Work your magic and let's hope like hell it works, because if not, we're all in deep shit."

CHAPTER THREE

WINSTON

I HATE PEOPLE.

I hate parties.

I especially hate being paraded around as man of the hour.

"It's your birthday," Nate says, clasping my shoulder and squeezing. "Lighten up. You're scaring all the hot chicks away with that mean mug of yours."

Lifting a brow, I smirk at my friend. "You do realize the 'hot chicks' I scared away with my glaring are Keaton's girlfriend and her posse."

Nate shrugs. "Still hot."

"And underage."

At this, he laughs. "If Ash were over there with them, just as young, your old ass would be over there trying to drag her into the nearest closet, laws be damned."

"Hmph."

"She's just a phase, right?"

My brow arches at his question. "Of course she is. They're all a phase."

That's all Ash is. That's all she can be.

"Right."

"You, of all people, should know this. You were there when…" I trail off, pinning him with a hard glare. Meredith destroyed me when I was a fucking teenager. Nate was there to remind me of who I am and who I'm meant to be. He knows I can't afford to put myself in that position ever again.

"Just looking out for you, man. I've always got your back." He cocks his head, frowning. "Where is Ash anyway?"

He scans the crowd of people milling around, chatting and laughing as they consume their champagne. She's not here. Neither are the Mannfords as far as I can tell. I know this because I've been hunting her down for the past hour and in that search, I haven't found them either. Too many fucking people.

"She'll be here," I mutter. "Hell, she may already be here."

The thought unnerves me. If those fuckers have her phone, she can't get into contact with me. I'm going to find them and wring their necks. When I see Perry's grinning face across the room,

I leave Nate to drool over the teenagers while I stalk my brother out. Along the way, every damn person wishes me a happy birthday. The party has barely started, and I'm already over it.

"Perry," I call out when I'm close. "A word?"

He excuses himself and saunters my way. His expression is unreadable, which is surprising. Whatever he's attempting to hide from me, I'll find out what it is. I gesture for him to follow me outdoors away from the suffocating crowd. Once outside, we skirt some people laughing in a group to stand near a shadowed area in the yard.

"What's going on?" I demand, piercing him with a firm glare.

His lips purse together as he darts his gaze around us. "I took care of it."

"It?"

He scrubs his palm over his face, a distressed glint in his eyes. "I don't know what happened."

"You're not making any sense."

"Ash," he hisses.

"What *about* Ash?" My voice is low and deadly. The hairs on the back of my neck stand on end. Not like I'm spooked, but more along the lines of a dog that's about to attack.

"She…" His features pinch in anguish. "They hurt her."

The blood running through my veins turns icy in an instant, hardening me to my very marrow. The pure cold whipping through me is hatred.

For them.

He doesn't have to tell me who because I already know.

The same motherfuckers who stole her phone.

"Hurt her how?" I demand through clenched teeth.

"I'm not sure. She's being tightlipped about it."

"Where is she?"

"I said I took care of it—hey, Winny, stop!"

I leave my brother as I storm back into the house, gaining momentum like an avalanche with every angry step along the way. I've just made it inside when Perry grabs my arm, stopping me.

"Wait," he bites out, his grip tightening when I try to shake him off. "What are you going to do?"

"It was her brothers, right?"

"*Step*," Perry bites out. "But yeah. She said it was them."

"Where is she?"

"She'll be here soon."

Our conversation is cut short when three

psychopaths in tuxedos approach. The ringleader—Scout—flashes me an evil grin. One that drips with triumph and power. Little shit doesn't know what he's started.

A fucking war he won't win.

"Constantine," Scout sneers. "Happy birthday."

"Children," I greet, making sure to look down my nose at them. "Where's your mommy?"

Scout's jaw clenches, and he narrows his gaze. "Better question is, where's *Winston's Dirty Whore*?"

Perry curses, stepping forward like he might deck this kid at Mother's ball. That's not happening on my watch. These shitheads would love for a Constantine to lose control. I shoot Perry a dark look that has him relaxing, letting me take the lead. Once I'm sure he's not about to knock Scout's head off, I step closer to the guy, loving that I outmatch him on height, weight, wits, and fucking money. I don't even have to remind him he's less than me. He knows it. He can feel it in the power of my gaze.

"Show him the picture, Sully," he grits out, not moving back.

Sully pulls out a phone, handing it to his brother. My nerves buzz, because I know he's about to show me something that's going to piss me off. Her phone is crammed with filthy shit we've done. This guy is going to throw it in my face, probably try to blackmail me. I know his type.

Hyenas.

Like Keaton said, we're lions, and I will pick this fucker's bones clean. In the figurative sense, though I wouldn't mind seeing him bloodied up by my fist. But that's not what hurts for little spoiled psychopaths. You don't beat the shit out of them. No, you shred their lives and the few things they care about. I already know I'm not going to be satisfied until I've ripped away everything that matters to him.

"I forgot to mention," Scout snarls, "my sweet sister won't be making it to your birthday ball, Constantine. She's had quite a bit of a dress fiasco."

I can intimidate most men with just a simple glare, but his words make my chest squeeze painfully. "Your taunting is getting boring, little boy. What do you want?"

"To warn you." His lips twist into a cruel smile that probably scares the shit out of his peers, but it only serves to infuriate me.

I arch a brow at him. "I'm a Constantine. We

don't take well to threats."

"Too fucking bad," he growls, thrusting the phone in my face. "This is only a taste of what I'm capable of." I realize it's not her phone, but it's a picture of her on it.

Ash.

My beautiful, wrecked, messy girl.

But not ruined by my hand.

No, this shit stain in front of me is responsible. He's desperate for my wrath—has a fucking hard-on for it. As much as I want to break the bones in his face with the phone, I school my explosive rage, containing it with a disinterested shrug.

"You can assault a woman half your size," I clip out, my eyes burning holes into him. "I see very clearly what you're capable of."

A waiter stops to offer champagne. I grab two glasses, handing one to Perry. My brother is watching me like a hawk, barely containing his own anger, but taking a page from my book and keeping it in check.

The psycho triplet twats are seconds from exploding.

I guess they're used to getting their way.

But I'm not a little girl or their motherfucking mommy.

I'm a goddamn Constantine.

And I *always* get my way.

Right now, I want to see them lose *their* shit. They think they've won, but they've only caught me off guard. As soon as I can, I'm going to upend everything in their world. Hell, I'll destroy Manda while I'm at it if I have to just to get through their thick skulls that fucking with Constantine property is a big, big no-no.

"We know all the sick shit you and Ash do together," Scout snarls, his face turning crimson as he poorly attempts to rile me up. "We know you pay her for it too."

I smirk at him and then quickly down my champagne glass before patting his chest. "You're going to have to do better than that, Mannford. Some filthy sex videos aren't going to bring down the king of this city. Try again, kid."

Sidestepping the brat, I make my way into the throng of people, my mind racing. Sure, I might not show Scout that he's ruffled me, but he has. Beneath the boiling of my blood is an innate urge to find Ash.

She'll be here soon.

I took care of it.

Through gritted teeth, I hiss at my brother. "Start talking and fast."

"She's here," Perry assures me. "Jac and Gus are getting her ready."

As though I have a sixth sense when it comes to Ash, my eyes weave through the crowd, seeking her out. I find Keaton walking in with Tinsley, but Ash isn't with them.

My sister, always the belle of every ball, prances forward in a blue dress that sparkles and moves like water as though she's wading through cerulean waves.

It's not Tinsley.

The fierceness emanating from the blonde is not my baby sister. It's a familiar one I know intimately. Lifted chin. Steady feet. Not an ounce of hesitation as she parades in on my little brother's arm pretending to be a Constantine.

How she managed to transform from the ruined, debased girl on her bedroom floor to a princess is beyond me. Perry has something to do with it, and apparently Keaton and Tinsley as well. I'm not sure what the young Constantines are up to, but for once, I'm grateful they've seemed to band together on my behalf.

It's because they know.

Ash is mine, and those triple fuckwads messed with what's mine.

My toy. My employee. My investment.

If Dad taught us anything, it's family above everything, even money. They've chosen to help me while not even knowing the full story.

What is *the full story, Winston?*

As much as Ash would love to be in on my inner monologue to somehow prove I've fallen for her, it isn't true. She's merely something that belongs to me, and I'm far too spoiled to allow other *children* to play with what's mine. That's all this is. Me being territorial over something I've invested time in and paid dearly for.

"You have her until midnight, brother," Perry says, squeezing my shoulder.

"What happens then? Does Cinderelliott turn into a pumpkin?"

He chuckles. "No, that's when Mother will turn into an evil queen if she discovers an imposter playing the part of her daughter."

Ahhh, the toasts.

"Let me guess. I'm supposed to play the charming prince until then."

"Nah, Winny, you were born to play the villain. And after what those fuckers did to her, charming is the last thing we need from you right now."

CHAPTER FOUR

ASH

B REATHE.
Don't panic.

I swallow down my unease, glancing over at Keaton. His features are cool and impassive, but he's tense. Much like Winston, I can tell Keaton wears his lack of emotion like a suit of armor, but if I had to guess, deep down, he has feelings too. It was evident he was unsure about leaving Tinsley and escorting me instead. Her relief was palpable and what seemed to push Keaton forward. It's heartwarming to feel their sibling connection.

"What now?" I ask, my voice slightly shaking.

"We avoid the piano room as that's where Mother will have taken up residence with her friends." He stops abruptly and guides me to the right. "It'd be best if we avoid my friends as well."

My heart flutters with nerves. "And my family too."

His piercing blue eyes meet mine and he studies me. "The Mannford triplets did something to you?"

"Just being themselves," I mutter. "They surprised me. It won't happen again."

He seems pleased by my answer and guides me onto the dance floor. It reminds me of my high school prom a few months ago. Tate was a perfect gentleman. Life felt safe with him.

And you never liked it.

I ignore the little voice inside me that reminds me I prefer quite the opposite. My relationship with Winston proves that tenfold. Everything about him screams unsafe, and yet I'm enamored by his wickedness. Turned on by his seductive cruelty.

A man with dark hair and dark eyes stares openly at me. For a second, I falter, worried that Leo Morelli has shown up at this party. Fear claws up my throat and makes me dizzy. When I suck in a deep gulp of air, my terror dissipates as I realize the man isn't a Morelli. With as much as the Constantines hate the Morellis, there's no way Leo would show his face around here.

He told me not to tell Winston, but what if I did?

Win would protect me.

Right?

He could keep me safe, maybe, but the on-slaught Leo would bring onto his family and mine would be more than even a Constantine could defend against. My skin crawls at the idea of every single person I know finding out about what Winston and I do in our private time.

I'll figure something out.

Maybe I can make something up to keep Leo off my back until I find a way to tell Winston.

"Tell me about the triplets," Keaton says, bringing his large palm to my waist and clasping my hand in his, making all thoughts of the Morellis fade as I think about my awful step-brothers. "I want to know what we're up against."

He leads us into a dance that's effortless on his part. I stumble at first as we find our rhythm but soon are moving in tune with the classical melody.

"They're assholes," I mutter, frowning at him. "Spoiled ones."

His lips curl into a sinful grin. "So are the Constantines. Tell me what they love."

"Their mother." Mama's boys through and through. "Lacrosse. And their cars."

Blue eyes light up with mischief. "Thanks for the insight… sis. But now I have to go explain to my girlfriend why I'm dancing with a girl who's not my sister. Based on the look on her face, she knows you're not Tinsley. Good luck."

Before I can process his abandoning me, another Constantine swoops in. Perry. His handsome grin calms me. Just like with Keaton, we easily fall into a rhythm that feels practiced.

"You might fool the outsiders, but anyone who knows Tinsley knows you're not the same. The hair and dress might play the part," Perry says, lifting a hand to tug on a blonde strand, "but you're as different as night and day."

"Different how?"

Perry studies me for a beat. "Tinsley is mostly good."

"I'm good," I argue to which he smirks.

"Sure you are." He winks, and I flush as images of last night with Winston that were definitely far from good flood my mind. "She's probably the nicest Constantine."

"I don't know," I argue. "You're my favorite so far."

He laughs. "I thought Winston was your favorite."

"Winston is… something. Favorite is a stretch."

His features pinch. "I know what the triplets did to you."

"They told you?" I meet his gaze, a lump in my throat.

"I saw a picture." A dark scowl transforms his face. "If Winny wasn't there, I'd have knocked that fucker's head off his shoulders."

"Picture?" I croak out. "He showed you a picture?"

"Don't worry," he assures me. "They won't get away with this."

Relief floods through me. I don't want them to get away with what they did. Even if it means I'll owe Winston and his family, I don't care. I want Scout and his brothers to be punished.

"Thank you," I murmur. "Where's Winston?"

"Rubbing elbows." He chuckles. "His favorite thing to do."

The idea of Winston schmoozing is definitely laughable. I can imagine him caught in conversation with his mother's friends, glaring at them. It makes me miss him. I've been in such a rush to get over here and ready that I didn't have much time to think about anything else.

"May I have this dance," a deep voice croons.

Just not *the* voice.

Disappointment trickles through me as I force a smile for Winston's friend, Nate. He's not staring at me like I'm a gold-digging whore, so I count it as a win in my book.

Perry gives me a nod of his head, indicating I'll be fine with Nate, and then passes me off to him. Nate grins at me as he settles his hand on my waist.

"A blonde now, huh?" His brow arches. "A new kinky game you and the boss man play?"

"Something like that," I lie, flashing him a fake smile. "Where's Winston?"

"Making an appearance with his mother." His eyes drop to my chest, lingering on my cleavage. "You do know his allegiance is first and foremost to his family, right? Your silly ideations of becoming his wife are nothing but childish fantasies. Winston will never settle, much less with a maid."

A maid?

I'm *so* much more than that.

"For as much as you worry over Winston's future, I'd say it seems as if you have a vested interest in it." I give him a bitchy smile. "Are we competing for his love? Because, Nate, I can assure you, there's nothing I won't allow that man to do if he asks."

Winston may not care about me the way I do about him yet, but I'll be damned if I let this prick intimidate me.

Nate misses a step and then stops, scowling at me. "It won't last. You're something that has his interest for the time being, but soon he'll grow bored of you. I'm his best friend. Those don't go away when the boner does."

I open my mouth to toss out something witty, no doubt, but then the vultures swoop in as soon as Nate walks away, rendering me speechless. It's Scout who pounces, though, while the other two linger like guards protecting their king.

"Let go," I hiss, attempting to pull my hand from Scout's grip.

"Not a chance, little sis," Scout growls, his strong fingers biting into my hip. "You're going to tell me how you pulled this off. The last time I saw you, you looked like shit. We made it that way."

I try to yank my hand from his grip, but he only tightens it, violence gleaming in his stare. But, unlike at home when I was at their mercy and alone, I face off with the monster, thankful to have witnesses.

"I'm resourceful," I spit out. "You may have robbed me blind, assaulted me, and threatened me, but surely you didn't think I'd roll over and take it, did you?"

"Maybe we weren't clear enough—"

His words are cut off as his eyes narrow behind me. We'd barely been dancing, but now we're at a complete stop. As soon as a chill shivers down my spine, I know why.

Winston.

Cold and domineering and arrogant.

His frigid authority warms me to my toes. I crave to fall back against his solid chest, allowing him to hold me in his protective arms. Instead, I suck in a sharp breath and wait out the staring contest between Scout and Winston.

"Run along, brats," Winston growls. "The adults need to talk."

Scout's nostrils flare, but he won't let me go. "Fuck you."

Winston steps closer until his chest is pressed against my back. "Do not make me say it again, or I'll embarrass the shit out of you in front of everyone here."

Sully grabs Scout's shoulder, but he shakes it off, fury rippling from him. He releases his hold on me and steps back.

"See you later, sis," Scout bites out, the threatening promise of more a thick, cloying malevolent fog around us.

The triplets storm off, disappearing into the crowd. Once it's safe, I turn around to face

Winston. The picture from earlier didn't do his appearance any justice. The man can wear a suit, that's for damn sure. But a tuxedo? He's delectable and dangerous all at once. A mix between prince and secret spy. A villain with a hero façade.

Tonight, in my story, he's more hero than villain. He chased away the monsters and stares at me like I'm the most beautiful thing he's ever laid eyes on. Sure, he's scowling because he's Winston freaking Constantine, but the intensity in his icy blue eyes is a mixture of concern and lust. It takes everything in me not to stand on my toes and press my lips to his.

"You have hearts in your eyes, Ash," he says with an arched brow. "Heart eyes mean you want flowery words, and you know those will cost you."

I deflate some, reminded of the fact those bastards stole all my money. "I can't afford them. I can't afford anything now."

The music changes to something familiar. Winston gets the devilish glint in his eyes right before he does something to thoroughly embarrass me. But, rather than feel apprehensive, I find comfort in it.

I thought my old boyfriend Tate was safe.

I was never safe with Tate, which was why he was easily run off by the Terror Triplets.

With Winston, I feel it. His dark unspoken promise shielding me from everyone around us. He'll want to make my stepbrothers pay for what they did.

"Dance with me." He offers me a hand. "Come on."

Lifting my chin, I meet his probing stare while not taking his hand. "How much?"

His eyes narrow, and his nostrils flare as he drops his hand. "It's my birthday. Shouldn't it be free?"

"The sex stuff is free," I say, tossing his own words back at him. "The rest has a price." I step closer and pat his chest. "Besides. I already got you a birthday present."

At this, he smirks. "What could my little maid have possibly gotten me?"

"You'll see. But first, let's make a deal. Five hundred per song."

"A grand if you stumble at least once over your own feet."

"I know how to waltz, Win," I huff. "It'll be harder to mess up on purpose."

"You've never waltzed with me, Cinderelliott. Take the deal or don't."

"You're lucky I need money," I sass back.

His villainous smile tosses a match on my

brittle heart, setting it on fire. "Indeed. Hurry, Ash, the song's almost over."

"Sweeten it for me, and you have yourself a deal."

"Since your poker face sucks, and I know you're better at dancing than I'm giving you credit for, I'll pay you two grand per song if you don't mess up."

I stick my hand out to shake on it. His hand envelops mine, offering me his strength. The song changes to "Unchained Melody" by The Righteous Brothers. He doesn't drop my hand, but instead wastes no time pulling me to him. Because he's Winston and waiting for me to goof up, I throw myself into the dance, recalling every dance lesson as a child and pre-teen. We effortlessly glide through the crowd, moving this way and that way until we've created a wide berth around us filled with smiling partygoers as they watch the birthday boy dance. It's a little unnerving, but I focus on the extremely successful and wickedly handsome man.

His stare is intense as he keeps his attention focused solely on me. He spins me out and then brings me back to him, neither of us losing stride. I gasp when he dips me, worried my wig might slip, but then he's tugging me back upright and all is well with my hair. We waltz around the room with practiced ease. Soon, the song is ending, but he doesn't let me go.

"Again?" he asks, his brow arched.

"Again."

His eyes linger at my mouth, and then we're dancing to something different. Thankfully, several people have joined us on the dance floor, including Keaton and his date.

"You'll have to pay me in cash until I can get a new phone sorted," I tell him. "Mine's gone."

A flash of fury darkens his blue eyes. "Shall I get it back for you, princess?"

I roll my eyes, fighting a grin. "You're supposed to capture the princess, villain, not try to defend her honor."

"Apologies, Cinderelliott, I have my tales confused."

"They took it all, Win." My bottom lip trembles once. "What they did to my dress…" I swallow hard, blinking back my tears. "It was horrible." Leo Morelli's terrifying scowl flashes in my mind, making me shudder. I wish I could tell Win there are more monsters in my world than the triplets, but I can't. I'm too scared, too worried that Win would… No, he wouldn't cast me aside for it. My heart seems to trip over itself at the thought, at the fear.

He gives me a clipped nod of his head. "It won't go unpunished. Now isn't the time. When you dive into a sea of sharks, you mustn't bleed. Not even a drop, because they'll sniff it from a mile away."

No tears.

No weakness.

I lift my chin, forcing a smile. "Did you know Perry has an orange car?"

At this, Winston laughs. Such a beautiful, rare sound. I could bottle it up and listen to it always. "Is that why Mother was all up in arms?"

"It's… special." I grin at him. "He loves it though. Threatened to make me walk if I didn't stop making fun of it."

His expression grows serious. "Speaking of, I owe you a car."

"Winston," I scoff. "You don't owe me a car."

It's a bitter reminder of what this is to him. A transaction. A game. Something to pass the time. For him, it's a way to spend his endless supply of money and find entertainment. For me, it's becoming so much more. Sometimes, though, when I stare deep enough into his cold blue eyes, I find warmth for me that gives me hope.

I have to believe we're more.

Even if I have to believe it for the both of us.

"I *do* owe you a car. I promised you last night." He stops as the song ends, eyes boring into me. "And you owe me a blowjob."

"If you please me at the birthday bash, I'll reward you with my dick down your pretty throat."

"Are you saying I please you?" I taunt, grinning at him.

His lips twitch. "You're too poor right now for my praise. I've raised the price anyway."

"You're such a dick."

"One you want to worship." He flashes me a wolfish grin. "Come on. I know a place where you'll get your filthy wish."

CHAPTER FIVE

WINSTON

IT TAKES EVERYTHING in me not to grab Ash's wrist and drag her through the hundreds of people until I have her alone in some dark corner. Instead, I offer my elbow—because I'm a fucking gentleman—and escort her away from the dancing people toward the kitchen. People continue to stop me and wish me a happy birthday, much to my annoyance. Ash sniggers under her breath each time I let out a curse when another person swoops in on me. Several of them eye Ash with curiosity while a few actually call her by my sister Tinsley's name.

What I'm about to do to her, though, isn't very brotherly.

We finally make it to the kitchen, and I walk her past the harried waitstaff. A few workers throw us confused looks, but no one argues.

"Where are we going?" Ash asks as I drag her down a quiet hallway.

"Someplace private."

I open the storage pantry and tug her inside before closing the door behind us. Her hazel eyes burn into me, and she licks her lips.

"What now?" Her voice is low and husky, serving to get my dick painfully hard.

"Now you get on your knees like a good little girl."

Her sassy eyebrow hikes up, but she starts to obey. I halt her, gripping her blonde locks.

"Not looking like my fucking sister." I pull off the wig and toss it onto the shelf beside me. "There. I prefer you a mess anyway."

Rather than be insulted, she gives me her famous heart eyes, grinning wide and happily. Girl is twisted as fuck because she enjoys my cruelty just as much as she likes my forced praise.

"I missed you," she says, standing on her toes to press a kiss to my lips.

Gripping both sides of her head, my fingers spearing into her frizzy, pinned hair, I devour her with a claiming kiss—one I've been dying to do all night. My sweet Cinderelliott tastes like cherry Starburst and sinful promises. All sweetness melts away as she tugs on my bottom lip with her teeth, her hazel eyes gleaming with wickedness.

"A grand if you let me shoot it on your face,"

I say with a smirk. "Let me paint your pretty eyelashes, beautiful."

The girl predictably preens at my words. "Five, and I'll let you take a picture."

"I surely thought you'd be spooked from photographs since our previous ones fell into the wrong hands," I taunt. "It seems I created a filthy monster who doesn't care about consequences, though."

"You did," she sasses. "Plus, I really need the money, Win. A girl's gotta eat."

I grip her shoulders and guide her to her knees. The miles of blue fabric from her dress pool around us as though we're standing in a blue lagoon of tulle. "I'll feed you."

She rolls her eyes. "Spoken like a true man."

A laugh snorts out of me. "You won't be eating my cock, little girl, you'll be gagging on it. Huge difference. I meant I'll take care of you."

A pregnant pause fills the air, and I realize it sounds a lot more prince-like and charming than I intend. She's my asset. My toy. Mine. And I need to keep her fed and safe if I want it to stay that way.

"You know what I mean," I grumble, unable to keep from stroking a stray hair away from her eyes. "Don't worry about cars or food or clothes or college. As long as we're playing our games, you'll be provided for."

She unzips my zipper and searches out my aching dick. Once she has it uncovered from my boxers, she pulls it through the hole. It looks obscene with her in her fancy dress on her knees with my dick bobbing out of the zipper hole in my slacks, the tip glistening with pre-come.

"I read up on this," she teases, gripping my fat cock in her small hand.

"Massive dicks?"

She laughs and fuck if my chest doesn't squeeze. "No, dummy. What we are."

"Wicked?"

"I'm your sugar baby."

I smirk at her, tightening my grip in her hair. "Stop talking, Ash, and choke on my dick. *Sugar baby.*"

Her nostrils flare like she might have more to say, but then I use the tip of my dick to paint my need along her juicy pink lips that fucking sparkle. She flicks her tongue out because she's greedy to taste me. I caress her head before pushing my dick past her lips, eager to feel her tongue on the underside of my shaft.

"Ommm," she murmurs in some strange sound of satisfaction.

I flex my hips, immediately hitting the back of her throat. She predictably gags and pulls back. My fingers twist into her hair, my only warning, before I press forward again. Her teeth scrape along my sensitive flesh, but the threat of pain isn't enough to outweigh the need I have to feel the inside of her throat as it constricts around me.

"Let me in," I growl, reveling in the choked gagging sound she makes.

Hazel eyes meet mine as she attempts to relax her throat for me. I like her looking up at me, so I grip her hair and bore my gaze into hers. Without preamble, I thrust my hips, cursing as the tip of my dick slides down the back of her throat. Tears well in her prettily made-up eyes, threatening to fall and ruin all Jac and Gus's hard work. I piston my hips again, going deeper.

"That's it, messy fucking girl," I croon. "So goddamn good to me."

Tears streak down her cheeks, dragging black mascara along with them, only serving to make her that much more beautiful. She gags again, her throat constricting around my dick in a way that has me seeing stars.

I fuck her face relentlessly, only pulling back enough to allow her to catch a breath every minute or so. Just as my nuts seize up with the need to come, I pull back, tugging on my cock as I find my release. Thick, hot ropes of come paint her forehead and cheeks, some of it dripping from her eyelashes.

Dirty, dirty girl.

"Gross, Win," she grumbles, her nose scrunching up. "I didn't think this through."

It's moments like these, that for one brief second when she's looking so fucking adorable, I imagine many, many more times like this for us. That is, until my mind catches up and reminds me she's my entertainment, not my future. My heart made a bad decision once before, and it nearly cost me my sanity. No matter how perfect she looks with my come all over her pretty face, it isn't enough to melt decades' worth of ice on my heart.

"Greedy, Cinderelliott. You were too desperate for that five grand." I smirk as I pull my phone from my pocket. "Say cheese."

She flips me off and sticks her tongue out, all of which only make me more amused and proud of our filthy pictures. Once I take a few to remember this moment, I put my phone away and pat her on the head.

"Good girl."

I help her to her feet, and she scowls, her

cheeks turning a pretty hue of pink. Tugging a handkerchief from my pocket, I set to cleaning the come off her face along with her streaked mascara. Once she's clean and I've shoved the soiled cloth into my pocket until I can toss it, I kiss her forehead. Her skinny arms wrap around my middle and she rests her cheek on my chest. My heart is still pounding from the epic blowjob. I wonder if she can feel how my heart thunders for her.

Fucking chump.

Your heart is stumbling all over itself because your old ass just blew your load all over a teenager's face. Legal teenager, but still young as fuck.

The small sigh of happiness that escapes her has my heart speeding up once more, and it has nothing to do with adrenaline.

It's her.

She's the drug, the addiction, the pulsing need.

I've never been addicted to anything in my life besides success. This overwhelming craving to consume every part of Ash is almost too much. It makes me feel weak. Like she's holding my balls in her prissy hand. All it would take is one squeeze to end me.

I tense, ready to grip her arms and pull her from my body, but her giggle has me taking pause.

"What?" I grind out as though I'm annoyed, though I'm smiling too.

"I was just wondering how long I could keep you captive in my arms before you made your great escape."

"You're playing me, little girl?"

She looks up at me, a brow arched high. "It's what we do, Win. We play."

"WHAT IS GOING on with your sister?" Mother demands, her voice low and only meant for me. "She's avoiding me."

I drain the rest of my champagne glass, setting it down on a nearby table, before glancing at my mother. "Elaine?"

Mother's lips purse together, her irritation bleeding through her veneered mask. "Tinsley. What's gotten into you, for that matter? I swear, every single one of my children is misbehaving tonight, and they all seem to be doing it as a combined effort to displease me."

"I assure you, no one is trying to displease you," I say, smirking at her. "Just let them be.

They're enjoying themselves tonight."

"Are you?"

"Immensely."

"I actually believe you, Winston," she says, suspicion darkening her eyes. "Question is, why? What do you have planned?"

"Nothing you need to worry about," I assure her with a brief smile. "If you'll excuse me, I need to run along." So I can track Ash back down, pry her from Perry's arms, and dance with her knowing I painted her pretty face with come not but a couple of hours ago. "There's someone I need to see."

"Actually," Mother says, her long fingernails biting into my bicep over my tuxedo jacket. "Stay, darling. We have some catching up to do."

The predatory glint in my mother's stare has my hackles rising. I know who it is before I even turn around because I recognize the perfume. I pin my mother with an accusatory glare. Her charming smile is in place, but I don't miss the calculation behind her pleasant features, and it doesn't involve me. Well, not directly anyway.

This isn't a betrayal.

It's a strategic move.

Swiveling around, I face the firing squad with the coolest expression I can muster.

My ex.

The one who ruined me when I was soft and weak and fucking vulnerable.

I really should thank her. She created the man I am today. Because of her, I forged iron around my heart, buried it beneath granite, and sealed it with a lock bigger than the fucking moon. I'm hard because she made me hard.

And not in the good way either.

But it's because of her that I am forced to deny myself certain things. Like Ash Elliott. Sure, I have her in every sense of the word, but not the way I'd like. I don't own all of her, not yet. Because I can't. I never can. The woman before me is proof of that.

Meredith is stunning perfection as always—silky blonde hair, paid-for tits, tight red evening gown that hugs her hourglass figure. It's not like I haven't seen her since our teenage breakup. Our families run in the same circles. It's just difficult seeing her in our domain. As though she belongs.

She never belonged, and my parents knew it.

"Meredith," I greet, my tone cold and uncaring. "Lovely seeing you here."

Duncan Baldridge, her husband whom I very much enjoy fucking over on the regular, juts his hand out and shakes mine. "Happy birthday, man. We were surprised by the invite, but we wouldn't miss it for the world."

Because who doesn't want to feast with the lions?

They're all here. The hyenas like the Mannfords and the snakes like the Baldridges. I'm sure lurking not far from the compound, the Morelli rats are salivating and wishing they were here too, gobbling up whatever crumbs we drop at our feet.

I catch Keaton's smirk from nearby, his rich girlfriend hanging off his arm, dripping in diamonds. I've often wondered why Mother plays this game with him. Positioning him with another successful family. Because it really fucking failed with me and Meredith. I'd thought I'd done the right thing dating someone in our social circle, but also falling for her too. In our world, it's one or the other in these arrangements. Convenience or love, but never both. Mother gladly exposed what a traitorous bitch Meredith was, saving me from a horrible mistake. She hasn't tried to set me up with anyone or push me toward any women since. Perry came along, and she let him be as well.

But Keaton…

Tearing my stare from my brother, I glance

over at my mother, my brow raised in question. Mother steps forward, looping her arm around mine as she smiles at Meredith.

"You've had work, dear," Mother purrs. "Fancy."

Meredith preens, making sure to bounce slightly so we all see exactly where she had her work done. "Thank you, Mrs. Constantine. It was a birthday gift from my Duncan."

Duncan, the dumb fuck, puffs his chest out like he performed the goddamn surgery himself rather than giving her the black AMEX card.

"Is your doctor taking on new patients?" Mother asks, her polite tone masking her true intentions.

"I think she'd make room for a Constantine," Meredith gushes. "Dr. Mannford is a friend of mine. I'll put in a good word."

"Dr. Mannford?" Mother gasps. "Well, what a lovely coincidence. She's a guest here tonight. Perhaps we should let the boys discuss whatever it is boys do and go have a chat with the talented doctor."

Meredith pokes out her bottom lip in a move that once had me vowing to do just about anything for her. "Promise we can catch up soon, Winston." She flashes me a wide grin before leaning in to press a kiss to my cheek, her new, talk-of-the-party tits pushing into my chest. "Happy birthday."

I refrain from rolling my eyes and keep my expression cool. As they walk away, my eyes lock onto Ash from across the room. Her hands are on her hips, and she's scowling after Meredith.

Jealous.

Cute.

I can work with that.

"Duncan," I say, turning to the ruddy-faced, prematurely balding guy who rubs me the wrong way every goddamn time I look at him. "I've been meaning to meet up with you."

"Oh?"

"I'm sad to say, but I made an error and let the Baldridge building go."

He blinks in confusion. "My building?"

It's mine, motherfucker.

"When you own as many as we do, sometimes things get lost in the shuffle." I frown at him. "I hope you're not angry."

He's more than angry.

He's volcanic.

His cheeks are redder than usual, and his thick neck is splotchy. I can practically see the steam pouring from his ears.

"How do we get it back?" he growls.

We.

Dumb fuck.

"This is where it gets terribly embarrassing," I say, pretending to wince. "I mistakenly sold it to a Morelli."

His face pales. "Y-You sold my family building to that trash?"

"Like I said, my mistake." I hold my palms up in a placating gesture. "But, as you know, nothing is final in this world. If you want something badly enough, you fight for it."

My eyes catch Ash's again. She's still glaring daggers at Duncan's bitchy wife.

"How do we get my building back?" Duncan asks, tugging at his bowtie. "Who knows what the Morellis will do with the tenants there. We have to take action."

Duncan forgets *he's* a tenant too, and no matter who's on the deed, the building will always be mine.

"How well do you know the other businesses in that square?"

He straightens his spine. "Well."

"Good." I give him a conspiratorial smile. "How about we sneak off and talk business?"

His eyes widen as though I've offered him a

golden goose egg.

No, fuckface, I'm using you.

"Lead the way, Constantine."

CHAPTER SIX

ASH

T HE WOMAN WORKS the room as though she belongs here. As though she's a Constantine. Sure, she even looks the part with her silky blonde hair and gorgeous body, but I can see right through her façade. At first, I was peeved off at the way she was looking at Winston. Like he belonged to her. But then, I sensed the disgust from him.

"Meredith Baldridge."

Perry's deep words only solidify what I saw in Winston's gaze. Not just disgust but regret and betrayal. She's the one who broke Winston's heart when he had one. Seeing her close to him, touching him, was enough to have me wanting to flaunt the fact that I have him now, and I'm not going to carelessly discard him like she once did.

"Come on," Perry says, "let's dance."

He tugs me onto the dance floor, and I quickly push away my irritation, giving in to reciprocating Perry's silly grin. Truth is, I like Perry. Keaton and Tinsley too. Winston is a prickly cactus most of the time, and I really like him. My stomach muscles tighten with anxiety. Not only are my stepbrothers harassing me, but I also have to figure out a way to deal with Leo Morelli, because he's not just harassing me. Leo is after Constantine blood, which means Winston and his siblings would be affected.

I can't let that happen.

I won't let that happen.

Even if it scares the shit out of me. I'll think of something. I have to.

Ting! Ting! Ting! Ting!

"Shit," Perry curses. "It's Mother. Toast time."

One look at the large clock on the wall and I realize we've danced the evening away. I pull from Perry's hold, grabbing a handful of my dress, and hurry past the people crowding toward wherever it is their mother is about to give her toast. Along the way to the corridor, I spy Winston talking to some guy. His eyes latch onto mine a second before he starts my way. Not stopping to wait on him, I rush down the hallway, nearly running into someone as they exit the bathroom. Barely, I manage to sidestep them, but the wobble has me losing my balance. As soon as the strap on the shoe I'm wearing snaps, I realize I've broken it. A few more steps and I learn I can't even keep it on my foot. Quickly, I kick it off, never losing stride. Since the other heel is tall, I run lopsided down the rest of the hall and up the stairs. When I push into Tinsley's room, she's waiting, her face and hair party perfect.

"I'm so sorry," I blurt out. "I lost track of time."

Tinsley tosses her shirt and shimmies out of her shorts while I fumble with the zipper on the dress. I manage to yank it down and step out of it but not before tripping over the material and falling on my ass.

"Calm down," Tinsley says with a laugh. "It wouldn't be the first time I was late to a party. Breathe, Ash."

"I broke your shoe," I grumble, showing her my bare foot.

"I have others," she assures me with a twinkle in her blue eyes. "Did you at least have fun?"

My mind immediately goes to the pantry where Winston and I behaved very badly. Crimson licks over my bare skin, heating my cheeks. "Lots."

"Good. Don't be a stranger." She disappears

into her giant closet and a few moments later, she returns a few inches taller having put on heels. "Nice meeting you." With a quick wave, she slips out of the bedroom, leaving me alone.

I'm still sitting on the floor in my strapless bra and panties with one shoe on, my heart pounding in my chest when I hear a soft click. Snapping my head toward the door, I let out a breath of relief to see Winston standing there in all his villainous glory. He holds up my shoe.

"Lose something, Cinderelliott?"

"Don't you have to do toast time with Mommy?"

His eyes darken as they peruse my partly naked form. "Have a stumble?"

"You missed an epic fall. One you'd have paid good money for too."

He tosses the shoe aside as he prowls my way. My skin heats for a whole different reason than earlier from my embarrassing fall. Winston isn't a match of lust tossed on my papery thin resolve to be a good girl; he's a bomb with a short fuse, exploding whenever I'm near. I have to crane my neck back to see his tall form as he stands over me, a gorgeous golden god whose interest has fallen to a mere mortal.

"I like seeing you like this," he rumbles, his

voice a deep timbre that rattles its way through my every bone.

"Looking like your sister?" I throw back.

His nostrils flare, and I laugh because I quite enjoy riling him up sometimes. He squats down in front of me, raising his hand like he might cradle my cheek. I lean toward his open palm and then cry out in surprise when he yanks my wig off. My eyes latch onto his lust-filled ones as he begins to roughly pluck pins from my hair, pulling strands from my scalp. Even though it stings, I like his undivided attention as he transforms me from someone meant to look like his sister back to his lover.

"What am I to you?" I ask, biting down on one corner of my bottom lip, searching his intense stare.

"Mine."

Pleasure floods through me, pooling in my pelvis. "Your what?"

"You're not rich enough for those words, little girl."

"I have a great job. I could earn the money pretty quick I'm sure."

He smirks. "Is that so?"

"I'm a hard worker, and I've learned to negotiate my salary."

"Why can't you just accept that you're mine and that's it?"

"Because you say it like one of your buildings. Or your cars. Or your watches." I wince when he pulls out pins close to my face. "I'm more than your property, Win, and you know it."

His blue eyes harden slightly. It's a punch to the gut, making me feel delusional. I'm positive he's not all granite and ice. Sometimes there's warmth. Sometimes he's human. I just have to work on pulling that side out of him more.

"Needy," he grumbles after he tosses the last pin away and scratches his fingers along my scalp, messing my hair up. "So fucking needy."

"Most girlfriends are."

"You're not my girlfriend."

"Basically."

He snorts. "We fuck, and I pay you to do demeaning shit. If you're my girlfriend, that makes me an asshole."

Apparently, I'm falling for one.

"Since when do you care about being an asshole?" I challenge. "Say it. Say, 'Ash Elliott is my girlfriend.'"

"No."

I make a face at him, dramatically rolling my eyes. "Whatever. I was willing to pay for it."

Would we be anything if we removed the money that binds us?

You can't purchase chemistry. You can't put a price on effortless conversation. I believe we can be. One day I'll prove it to him.

"You didn't make that much money down-stairs."

"I was going to barter."

His eyes darken. "I'll think up a fitting trade."

"I'll be ready."

He rises to his feet and then pulls me to mine. I let out a squeal when he throws me over his shoulder as though I weigh nothing, smacking my bare thigh hard. "I don't have time for this game, but rest assured, Cinderelliott, it will continue."

"Where are we going?" I demand as soon as he opens the bedroom door, my heart freezing in my chest.

"As much as I'd love to parade you around the party like this, I don't think Mother would approve. I'm taking you to my room here on the compound, and you'll wait for me where we'll continue our negotiations soon."

"I need my bag." I wriggle and try to point toward the sitting chair. "There."

He smacks my ass again, because he's a damn sadist and likes to hear me howl, and saunters over to it. After snagging it up, he totes me out of Tinsley's room and down the hallway. We eventually wind up in a room that is decidedly Winston's.

Dark navy walls.

Rich, modern wood flooring.

Sleek furniture and minimal décor.

It's cold and masculine, but somehow warms me straight to my core because his room here smells like him. He tosses me on the bed and sets my bag on the floor.

"I'll be back," he growls, his gaze sweeping over my breasts that have nearly fallen out of the top of the cups of my bra after our little jaunt. "Be ready for me."

He turns on his heel and starts for the door. Before he leaves, I call out, stopping him.

"Happy birthday, boyfriend."

His laugh barks out of him, warming me to my core. He flips me the bird and leaves without another word.

I grin like a damn idiot.

I'm in too deep with this man.

MY LASHES FLUTTER as fingertips dance over my ribs. I open my eyes to discover a shirtless

78

Winston stretched out beside me on the bed, his head propped up on his arm as he bores his stare into me. He's unusually quiet and seems to be studying me, so I take the moment to openly look at him. His dark, golden blond hair is no longer styled to perfection but damp from a recent shower. I fixate on his full lips that are usually spouting off cruel things but feel so good when they're on my flesh. Reaching up, I brush my fingertips over his mouth. He abandons my ribs to clutch onto my wrist, holding me in place.

"Are you okay?" I ask, frowning at him.

He parts his lips, sucking three of my fingers into his mouth. When he bites down rather painfully, I knee him in the thigh. His teeth release me, and he flashes his devilishly handsome but still super evil grin that promises torment.

"I'm fine now." He grips my thigh, hauling me closer. Then, his thumb traces over the Sharpie words that still remain on my stomach. I shiver at his touch. "Tell me everything."

My blood runs cold at his words. I'm disgusted and horrified at the way my stepbrothers treated me when they destroyed my dress, robbed me, and threatened me. Then, seeing Leo Morelli was the icing on the cake.

"Manda saw this," I say, gesturing to where

he's back to stroking my stomach. "Flipped out. Claimed I was going to destroy the family." I give a one-shouldered shrug. "I disgust her."

The way his heated gaze bores into me, I know for a fact Winston feels the exact opposite.

"Then, she left me with them." I swallow down my emotions, willing myself not to cry. "They mentioned Harvard."

Winston's eyes narrow. "I warned them. I don't make threats I don't carry out."

"Well, they blame me. Said I made you do it."

He's tense, but his touch is soft as he strokes my stomach. "Then what?"

"They stole all my cash. Forced me to unlock my phone and hand over my laptop password." Tears threaten, and I blink them away. "Took all the money in my account."

Winston is deadly still, the only signs of his emotions are the continuous ticking muscle on his jaw and the pulsating vein on his brow. He's great at seeming cool and collected when inside he's raging. The way his blue eyes burn into me, I'm practically scalded by his fury.

"Go on," he clips out. "Tell me what else."

"Held me down, cut my dress off, and threw me in the shower." A tear leaks out, running down my cheek and clinging to my jaw.

He reaches up and swipes at the tear, collecting it on his thumb before bringing it to his full lips. I track his movement as he sucks away the salty wetness. "Then what?"

I want to tell him about Leo Morelli, but Leo is different than my bully stepbrothers. Leo is dangerous. He's a Morelli, and from what I've gathered, they're like the mafia or something. The last thing I need is Leo finding out I told Winston when he expressly demanded I don't.

"There's nothing left to say." I slide my thigh over his hip, pushing him onto his back as I straddle him. "Now it's time for your birthday present."

His intelligent eyes inspect every part of me, searching for what I've left unsaid. The man's not the king of this city for no reason. He's on top because he's smart and nothing passes him by. I just need for him to not press. I'll figure something out. And who knows? Maybe Leo was all talk and no game. What I need to find out first is how he's connected to the Terror Triplets.

"Let's see what the poor maid bought her boss," he taunts, his fingers digging into my thighs as he roughly holds onto me.

"I didn't buy it," I sass back. "I made it."

He rolls his eyes, making him seem much

younger like Keaton. It makes me laugh. I reach over to the nightstand and grab the envelope off the top.

"Here."

"A gift card to Starbucks. How original."

I smack at his bare chest. "It's not a gift card, asshole."

He smirks as he opens the card. His brow lifts in question as he pulls out a handmade booklet. "Coupons."

I grin at him. "Cool, right?"

Ignoring me, he flips open the booklet. "A coupon for one free massage from Ash." His eyes dart to mine, amusement dancing in them. "I could go to the spa and get a massage from someone qualified."

"Would they do it naked?" I taunt.

"Hmm," is all he says as he flips to the next page. "Bedtime story by Ash. A bedtime story, huh? A story about the big, bad wolf with his dick up Goldilocks's ass?"

I cackle and smack him again. "You're an idiot."

He flips the page and shakes his head. "A free cuddle. I can assure you, I'm never using this coupon."

I pout, earning a smile from him. "You never

know. They don't expire so you're good there."

"You thought of everything, I see," he remarks, his eyes back on the booklet. "A trip to the candy store. Hmm."

"There's a really neat place where you can mix and match—"

"I don't eat candy," he interrupts, flashing me his perfect white teeth.

"Fine, we'll buy some for Perry. We're going and soon. I'm running low on cherry Starburst."

He flips the page. "Movie night in Winston's bed."

"Sounds fun, right?"

"All of this sounds like torture if we're being honest."

"But you love torture," I argue.

"When I'm the one doing the torturing." He tosses the coupon book away and grabs onto my neck, pulling me to him. "That was the most ridiculous gift I've ever received."

"You're welcome," I say with a grin.

His lips press to mine, and he kisses me like he's thankful for *the most ridiculous gift*. Since I was naked and waiting for him, it doesn't take long for him to shove his boxers down, freeing his thick, eager cock. Greedily, I slide up and down his length, letting him feel how hot he gets me.

His tongue spears into my mouth, and his grip on my ass is nearly painful. I arch my back, lining my opening up with the tip of his dick and then flex my hips so that he slides inside my body. With a hard thrust, he bucks into me. His fingers are going to leave bruises as he forcefully guides me to meet his rhythm. I pant heavily against his mouth, trying to keep up with his maddening pace.

"Oh god," I groan, grinding against him, loving how he hits me in all the right spots. "So good."

He pinches my nipple and twists it until I whimper. His lips pepper me with hungry, open-mouthed kisses along my jaw. When he gets to my throat, he sucks hard enough to make me gasp. With each powerful thrust up into me, I grow more and more dizzy by the need to come. Raking my nails over his chest, I revel in the sharp hiss that escapes him. He nips at my throat hard enough I cry out.

Mine.

I feel the word whispered over my flesh more than I hear it. It's enough to send me over the edge. Stars glitter around me as my orgasm tears through me, obliterating my every nerve ending. He comes with a growl that sets my soul on fire.

Heat floods into me, claiming me as his, just like he said.

I collapse onto his sweaty chest, breathing heavily. "How much to keep you right here for the night just like this?"

"Everything you earned tonight."

It's then, I realize we can do this. Without the money if we have to. I'd have to get a real job and an apartment, but we could still have this. We could keep our games and our fantastic sex and our teasing conversations. He's protective and caring and in tune with my needs.

I'm not Meredith.

I would take care of his heart, not break it.

He just has to let me inside.

"Deal." I stroke my finger over his shoulder. "Happy birthday, Win."

"Indeed it is, Cinderelliott."

I make him happy.

The billionaire who has everything finds enjoyment in the company of me. Some might say it's a fairy tale ending, but even I know Winston's no charming prince.

CHAPTER SEVEN

WINSTON

SOMETHING'S UP WITH my mother.

First, the party she insisted on throwing last night. Then, inviting Meredith, whom she hates with the fire of a thousand suns. Now, a quaint outdoor breakfast with all her children. She may be a master puppeteer, but no one pulls my strings, not even Mother. I want her to cut the shit and reveal whatever it is she's doing.

And, as soon as my mama's boy brother extricates himself from Mother's side, I'll lay into her and find out.

"That's why Perry will never get married," Keaton mutters under his breath. "He's such a pussy sometimes."

Perry catches us watching him, and he does a stupid chin lift, never slowing his conversation with Mother.

"Who says Perry even wants to get married?" I throw back at my little brother.

"It would please Mother; therefore, it would please him." Keaton smirks at me. "Oh, I found out some stuff about the triplets."

I lean over in my seat, interested in what Keaton's discovered. "I'm listening."

"They care about three things." He glances over at Perry again. "Their mommy, their cars, and lacrosse."

"Hmm."

"What are you going to do?"

"Take it all away and watch them cry."

Keaton chuckles. "Evil bastard."

"Says my protégé."

"I'm not your protégé." He slouches in his chair and starts texting, effectively ending our conversation.

"I like her," a voice to my left says.

Arching a brow, I smirk at Tinsley. "Get your own assistant."

"But I like yours."

A smile tugs at my lips as I ignore the baby of our family. I was a grown-ass man when she was born. Since she's the precious princess of the Constantine family and I'm tasked with keeping everyone fed, we don't cross paths much aside from our occasionally required meals with our mother and other functions. I do know that when it's time for her to date, I won't have to ward anyone unworthy off because Keaton will handle that just fine. He takes his protective role over her seriously. I envy their closeness.

Since fucking when, Winston?

Since Ash started poking at my frigid heart. The girl has figured out a way to get under my skin. Not many people are able to do what she's accomplished in just a few short weeks.

She gave me a damn coupon book.

I'm biting back a grin when Mother calls my name.

"Hmm?" I lift my gaze, wiping the smile off my face. "Did I miss something?"

"We were talking about my badass new car," Perry says, a goofy fucking smile on his face.

Keaton snorts, and Tinsley giggles. From across the table, Vivian smirks and even the perennially coked-out Elaine grins.

Mother is not amused.

"No," Mother says with a heavy sigh. "We weren't. I asked Perry why you sold the Baldridge building."

The table goes silent, each of my siblings curious of my answer. Only Perry knows why. I realize now he must have been trying to distract her from this conversation, because he seems exasperated at having failed.

"Business, Mother. Nothing to worry over."

"That's an evasive answer," she bites out. "Elaborate."

"I just felt like it," I growl, pinning her with a glare. "Drop it."

Her lips press together as anger flashes in her eyes. "I'm not one of your employees or one of your siblings, young man. I am your mother. Do not ever disrespect me like that again."

"And I would urge *you* not to disrespect my business decisions, *Mother*. This company wouldn't be exploding with growth if it weren't for the choices I've made. Even if you don't understand them."

Naturally, my answer isn't good enough based on her disappointed frown. It's as though she enjoys trying to make an ass out of me in front of my siblings—to remind everyone she's the queen of everything and we're merely her silly children.

I fucking own this city, and it's high time she realizes it.

"That was the only Constantine-owned building on that block," she continues as I knew she would. "Imagine my surprise when Anthony divulged to me you sold it to a Morelli." Anthony, my loose-lipped attorney and old friend of Dad's, will get his ass chewed out for tattling to my mother.

Elaine nearly knocks over her glass of water. "You sold our building to a Morelli? Which one?"

I briefly study my sister, curious as to why she's so fucking interested. Usually, she can't be bothered to look up from her phone.

"It doesn't matter. And in case you all forgot," I drawl out, turning my attention back to Mother, "I'm the CEO of Halcyon. That requires certain strategic moves. Have I not proven myself capable of taking care of this family?" She's seen the financial reports. She already knows the answer.

Mother's nostrils flare. "It's a simple question, Son."

"Mother, enough," Perry barks out, making everyone go quiet with shock at his outburst. "Winston knows what he's doing. Just trust him."

Her hardened exterior seems fractured at having been put in her place by the golden child. She frowns as she turns to Perry. Absently, she picks off a non-existent piece of lint from his wrinkled shirt. My mother is the proverbial ice queen, and like a queen, she chooses her battles wisely.

"You're right," she says to him. "Winston knows what he's doing. I would hope, though, that if he were ever in trouble, he would come to me. I have my ways."

"Did one of your ways involve inviting my ex-girlfriend?" I ask, coolly. "Imagine my surprise seeing Meredith at my birthday party."

Mother shakes her head and waves a dismissive hand my way. "Honestly, Son, it was nothing you need to worry about. I've taken care of you before regarding that woman, and I'd do it again."

The conversation shifts back to Perry's orange abomination of a car. Keaton leans toward me, chuckling. "Five bucks says Mother has a fleet of hitmen at her disposal."

"Who do you think pays them?" I ask, arching a brow at him.

"Touché." His eyes meet mine. "Where's your girlfriend?"

Not my girlfriend. Just mine.

"Naked and worn out in my bed. And she's not my girlfriend."

My little brother just laughs. Fucker.

"GET DRESSED," I bark out in greeting as I enter my room at the Constantine compound. "We have errands to run today."

Ash pauses mid-bite on the piece of buttered toast she's eating, and her brow arches. Then, she chomps down on the food, messily eating it as she rolls her eyes. After she swallows, she says, "Good morning to you too."

"You can play games when you can afford it. Right now, you're back to being the poor, unfortunate maid who needs the rich guy to save her. Get up, get dressed, and let's go."

I expect more argument, but all I get is the middle finger before she abandons the breakfast I had sent up by one of the kitchen staff. My gaze travels down the length of her curvaceous body, settling on her ass as it bounces with each step. I'm half hard and aching to fuck the sassy girl, but we have too much to do today. It'll have to wait. Leaning against the wall, I take to browsing through some pictures on my phone she'd sent me. The filthy ones do the job of making my dick completely hard, but it's the bratty ones that do something else.

That bitchy smile makes *me* smile.

"Planning world domination over there?" Ash asks around her toothbrush from the bathroom doorway.

"Just domination over you."

"Weirdo." She disappears back into the bathroom. After spitting and the water starts to run again, she says, "We have to check on Shrimp."

"I've taken care of it. Francis says the bird is fine."

She walks out of the bathroom dressed in holey capris and a white tank that's transparent, revealing a black bra underneath. It's borderline trashy but for some reason, I find it really fucking hot.

"This is all I brought with me," she says, frowning as I drink her in. "We can stop by your place if we need to and I can change."

"It'll be fine for the errands we need to run." I gesture at her messy hair. "Do something about that."

She narrows her eyes at me but doesn't snap back. Instead, she pulls a hair tie from her pocket and smooths her hair back into a high ponytail. Her hazel eyes drop to the way my dick strains in my slacks. "Maybe you should do something about *that*."

"That'll get taken care of later," I assure her. "Let's go."

Within ten minutes, we're walking through the expansive estate to the garage bays. Once inside the garage, I walk over to one of my cars I leave at the compound. My pearl-white Bugatti

Chiron. Earlier, I'd retrieved the keys from the safe in my room, so as we approach, I press the button on the fob making the doors lift up.

"Boys and their expensive toys," she teases, though I can tell she's impressed.

"You're one of my toys." I smirk at her. "Much cheaper than this one."

It's a good reminder for the both of us.

Constantines grow tired of their toys rather quickly if I'm being honest.

She'll learn that soon.

Liar.

"I've upped my price, Constantine. Don't worry. I'm worth it."

Her dazzling smile has my chest tightening. Ignoring the rush that floods my veins, I climb into the Bugatti. Once we're settled and buckled in, I fire up the engine. The car vibrates from the power of it. I back out of the garage and then peel out of the driveway, no doubt leaving tire marks that Perry will get blamed for. Ash is quiet, silently taking in all the sights as we make the drive back into the city.

"What kind of cars do the triplets have?" I ask, speeding past a row of slow drivers.

"Matching black Audis. Cute, huh?"

"Adorable." I glance over at her. "Their

mommy bought them?"

"Yep."

"Aren't you a part of the family? How come you don't have a matching Audi in pink?"

"Because I'm not a part of that family," she huffs. "Plus, I don't want to owe her anything."

"But you'll gladly owe me?"

"It's different with you. I feel like we're on equal footing."

I scoff at this. "I'm a billionaire, Ash. We're nowhere near equal footing."

"A billionaire who, for the right price, will happily spend his money on me. The strings attached are the ones on my terms. Ones I agree to. With Manda, it's the forever kind of strings. I hate owing her."

"Hmm."

"As much as you hate to admit, we're evenly matched, Win."

As traffic slows to a halt, I take my time perusing her. With the sunlight streaming in and kissing her golden skin, she's very much a vision. Real. Unlike any other woman I've had in my grasp before. Her innocence is charming, but it's only for my benefit. Beneath that façade is a filthy freak like me. So, maybe we are evenly matched where our sexual proclivities are concerned.

"Where are we going?" she asks when I pull up in front of a building.

"To get you a new phone. Stay here."

I'd called ahead, so as soon as I walk into the store, the manager meets me with the newest iPhone already set up and ready to go. This one is on my plan. After I program my number into it and text myself, I walk back outside and climb into my vehicle.

"Here," I state, thrusting the phone at her. "Send me a picture so I know it works."

The sassy girl makes a stupid duck face and then my phone buzzes in my pocket.

"I'm not paying for that picture," I say, smirking at her. "Which reminds me. Change your online banking password and set up Apple Pay on this phone."

"You're so bossy."

"I think you meant to say, 'thank you.'"

She leans over the console, grabs my tie, and pulls me to her. "Thank you."

I allow the greedy girl to kiss me for free, and then I pull away so we can head to our next destination. While she messes with the new phone, I ponder how I'm going to ruin the triplets' lives. I've already fucked up Harvard for them, but it's not enough. I hadn't been joking to

Keaton about Mother having hitmen, and I'm seriously considering tapping one. We have a meticulous list of the best killers money can buy. Those three little fuckfaces are polluting the goddamn planet with their toxic presence.

"You're growling," Ash says, jerking me from my internal thought. "I have an idea to make you smile, but it's going to cost you."

"Maybe I don't want to smile."

"Play along, Win, and I promise you won't be disappointed."

I lift a brow. "I'll bite."

"Get your coupon book out…"

"For fuck's sake, Cinderelliott."

But, because this girl has me all wrapped up in her and tangled in a fucking mess, I tug the coupon book from my shirt pocket and toss it at her.

"Now, try to take the stick out of your ass and enjoy this," she says, patting me on my thigh. "I'll make it worth it."

CHAPTER EIGHT

ASH

H E'S NEVER HAD candy.

What sort of horrible childhood did he have to endure growing up? I'm still reeling at his confession when we pull up to the shop my dad and I used to go to a lot after Mom died. It makes sense why he was so uninterested about my candy store coupon. I'm giddy at the prospect of getting to show him how much fun a candy store can be.

"I need to earn a few hundred bucks before we go inside," I tell him. "Tell me how."

His blue eyes are sharp as he sweeps his gaze over me. "Easy. Take off your bra."

"This tank is see-through," I argue.

"It's not my fault you chose that shirt. Want to make five hundred bucks or not?" He pulls his wallet from his slacks and flips it open, his eyebrow arching in that maddening challenging way that makes my blood boil.

"Fine. Give me all the money in your wallet

and I'll get rid of my panties too."

His gaze darkens. "Right here? With people walking by?"

"I'll be quick."

He chuckles, tugs the money out of his wallet, and tosses all the bills at me. They rain down into my lap, slide between the seat and the console, and onto the floor. Bastard. I take my time gathering them up and counting them. Eighteen hundred dollars. Worth it. I shove the money into my purse and then set to removing my bra. Once it's gone and shoved into my backpack, I unbutton my capris and slide the zipper down.

"Oh," I gasp, feigning surprise. "Where did they go? I must have done it already. My bad."

The shock that registers on his features is brief, but pride washes through me knowing I put it there, no matter how short a time.

"I see how it is," he growls, his hand smacking mine away. "Let me touch you right here, and I'll match the cash I just gave you with a deposit to your Apple Pay."

"Eighteen hundred dollars to finger me?" I let out a breathy laugh. "You twisted my arm. Okay."

His fingertips tease the skin on my lower belly before he pushes a finger between the lips of my pussy, sliding against my clit and making me jolt.

"You're wet. The idea of walking around a candy store with no panties on makes your pussy wet."

"It's the little things in life," I murmur, squirming at his expert touch.

"Hmm."

I bite on my bottom lip, suppressing a whimper when his finger dips inside me. He fucks it in and out slowly before smearing my arousal on my clit. My body is alive, jittery with the need to come. He rubs delicious circles around my clit, drawing me closer and closer to the edge. Just as I tense up, my release ready to explode, he pulls his hand away, leaving me hanging.

"Win," I whine. "What the hell?"

He rubs his wet finger across my bottom lip and then my top one. "Hmm?"

"I hate you."

"I love that you do."

Leaning forward, he kisses me hard, sucking on my lips so he can taste me from them. I groan when he bites on my bottom lip and tugs. His kiss is deep and consuming. I'm dizzied and disoriented by the time he pulls away.

"Fix your pants, little girl. We have to buy your bratty ass some candy."

Sighing, I fasten my jeans, shove Win's coupon book into his pocket, and then grab my purse before stepping out of the Bugatti. Winston strides over to me as the doors fall closed on his vehicle, looking like a million bucks in a new, fresh suit. Of course his bedroom at the compound was stocked with clothes and everything he might need. I have a feeling wherever Win goes, he's always prepared.

I grab his hand, threading my fingers with his.

He falters, his brows furrowing. Except with me. He's prepared for everything and everyone in this world, but not when it comes to me. The fact I can rattle the poised, elegant Winston Constantine is empowering.

"Hand holding will cost you," he complains but doesn't fight me off.

"I'll buy you some candy. Don't worry."

Ignoring my smartass remark, he opens the shop door and ushers me inside. It's exactly as I remember, bustling with families, floor-to-ceiling shelves of candy, and a giant center island with self-serve machines of various candies. Winston is stiff as he follows me inside, clearly uncomfortable at being here.

"First off, we need to get what we came here for," I tell him, making a beeline straight for the cherry Starburst machine. I grab a bag and hold it under the spout, twisting until I've filled it with my favorite candy. Once I tie it off, I hand it to him to hold. "What kind of candy do you want?"

"I told you," he grumbles, "I don't eat candy."

"Too bad," I throw back. "Today you're going to eat some. Question is, what will Winston Constantine like?"

He rolls his eyes at me but continues to follow me throughout the store. I make sure to collect a variety of my favorites for him to try. When I find him eyeing the gummy bears with curiosity, I call over a salesperson.

"Excuse me," I say to the young woman. "Can he have a sample?"

She frowns. "Of gummy bears?"

"He's never had one."

A gasp tumbles out of her lips. "Seriously?"

He ignores us. Asshole.

"Seriously. Give him a red one. I know for a fact he's a fan of cherry." I make a great show of winking at him, earning a smirk.

The girl, using her gloved hand, pulls out a couple of red ones and hands them to me. As soon as she walks off, I step close to Win, grinning at him.

"Open up," I tease.

He scoffs but then obeys. I push the gummy into his mouth, watching him intently to see his expression. Slowly, he chews, frowning hard. After he swallows, I feed him the other one. Once that one is gone too, I bounce on my toes, unable to keep still.

"So?"

"So what?" he grumbles.

"What do you think?"

"They're chewy. A lot of work to eat."

"You're not lazy, Win. What about the taste?"

"Tastes like you." His blue eyes sear into me. "They'll do."

In Win speak, he loved it. Ha! I knew it. Luckily, at this candy store, the gummy bears are sorted out by flavor. I dump a bunch of red ones into the bag and then continue down the way. Once I've gathered as much of a variety I can think of, even some old man stuff like chocolate-covered coffee beans and saltwater taffy, we make our way to the register. He goes to pull out his wallet and I shake my head.

"Use your coupon," I tell him, enjoying the way his cheeks turn slightly pink at the word coupon.

"You have a coupon, sir?" the cashier asks.

"No," he barks out. "She's being a brat."

Confused, the cashier goes back to silently ringing us up. I reach into his pocket, flip to the candy store coupon and rip it out before depositing his booklet back into his pocket. He watches my movements with a narrowed glare that makes my body burn hot. When his eyes settle on my breasts, I'm reminded that I'm not wearing a bra. Thankfully, it was too busy in here for anyone to notice.

The cashier tells me the total, ending our silent staring. I fish out some cash and pay for all the candy. Once she hands me the bulging sack, I grab Win's hand and pull him back outside.

"Are you happy?" he complains.

I stand on my toes, kissing him with tongue. Tasting the cherry gummy bear in his mouth has me smiling. "Very much so."

"Let's get going then. We have to go pick up your car."

✧ ✧ ✧

WE ARGUED THE entire way to the Cadillac dealership. Seriously. He's buying me a car. Or, according to him, already bought it and just needs to pick it up.

"Why can't you just drive me everywhere? I'm not even that good of a driver and will probably wreck it."

"Stop whining." He flashes me an evil smirk.

"Don't worry, little girl, it'll be the safest vehicle for you."

He pulls up next to a souped-up black Cadillac Escalade. I'm thankful it's not anything ridiculous like a Lamborghini or a Bugatti.

"Let's test it out," he says once he turns off his car.

I clamber out and follow him over to the massive beast of an SUV. It seems bigger than a normal Escalade. A sales guy greets Win and tosses him the keys. I'm forced into the driver's side after dumping my bags into the backseat, and Winston climbs into the passenger side.

"This thing is huge," I complain. "I'll probably sideswipe every car I pass."

He relaxes in his seat, unperturbed by my threats. "It's an armored vehicle. It'll survive."

"What?"

"To keep you safe."

"An armored vehicle like those trucks that carry money?"

He scoffs. "Don't be silly. This is a lot more expensive than one of those. More like the type of armored vehicle that transports the president."

"Winston," I groan. "Why are you so over the top?"

"It's my money. I can spend it however I

want."

I try not to melt at the fact he bought me an armored vehicle to keep me safe. I'd assume his intentions were honorable except he has a devilish glint in his blue eyes.

"Where to?" I ask, huffing.

"By my place so you can change into something more appropriate." His grin turns wolfish when my cheeks burn hot. "And then we'll have a bite to eat."

"What then?"

"We'll set off to check off another item on my list."

"Why do I feel like I'm about to be an accomplice in a crime?"

His deep, throaty, and super evil laugh doesn't help calm my fears. "No, Cinderelliott, you have that quite backwards. Today, I'm *your* accomplice."

I shouldn't trust the devil in a three-piece suit.

Unfortunately, I do.

"Better be worth it." I shoot him a narrowed glare.

"Oh, it will be. You'll see."

CHAPTER NINE

WINSTON

H ER MOUTH DRIVES me wild.
The things it can do. The words that spill out. The taunting smiles.

I've never had a woman who edges me toward the cliff of insanity like Ash Elliott does. At one time, I'd have balked at seeing a woman like her. Now, I can't imagine seeing anyone but her. The thought is alarming, and frankly, embarrassing.

She's. My. Plaything.

Keep telling yourself that, asshole.

Ignoring my inner berating that sounds like it might be in Perry's voice, I tear my gaze from her mouth where she'd been licking her lips after a bite of the chocolate cheesecake she's been eating. Earlier, we went by my place so she could change and play with her loud-ass bird. Then, I took her to one of my favorite restaurants in town. Even when she's not embarrassing herself for my pleasure, I still enjoy her company.

Fucking chump.

"You're brooding," Ash says, her hazel eyes boring into me. "You okay?"

"I'm perfectly fine," I lie, not meeting her gaze. "Are you going to make love to that cheesecake all night or are we going to leave already?"

The brat takes an exaggerated bite of her dessert, moaning loudly for all to hear. My dick perks up, enjoying the hell out of her husky sound of pleasure.

"Want to earn fifty grand?"

She nearly chokes on her cheesecake. "Fifty?"

"Yes or no, little girl?"

"Yes," she says without hesitation. "What sort of fucked-up stuff are you thinking?"

I admire her pretty, plump lips for a beat. "I grabbed this from home. I want you to put it in." Pulling her jeweled butt plug from my pocket, I set it down on the table with a loud thunk.

Her eyes widen, and she snatches it off the table. "Like right here? I can't do that here!"

A dark chuckle escapes me. "Of course not, dirty girl. Go to the bathroom and put it in. Send me a picture once it's done."

"That's it?"

"I'm not done," I say, my gaze dragging down

her creamy throat to her cleavage. "While you're gone, I'll move to one of those booths at the bar. Come back and sit on my lap."

"Oh god," she groans, her eyes wide with apprehension. "And then?"

Smart girl.

"If you fuck me without drawing attention to us, you'll get your money."

"Here? In the restaurant? Are you insane?" she demands, her hazel eyes flaring with shock.

"Not here. At the bar. And, yes. Positively insane." *For you.*

Dumbass, motherfucking chump.

"That's all? For fifty grand, I put my butt plug in and secretly fuck you at the bar?" When I nod, her features turn wicked. "I'll knock off ten if you use one of your coupons later and tell me how much you need me in your life while we watch a romantic movie."

A laugh barks out of me. "No."

"Fifteen off?"

"No. Fifty. No coupons and no sweet words."

"No deal." The bratty girl even crosses her arms over her chest in a petulant way to drive home her words.

"Fine, Cinderelliott. Fifty and I'll use the stupid-ass movie night coupon later. And, I'll tell you how much I need you right after."

"But?"

"But I get to say degrading shit to you while we fuck."

"Fine," she huffs. "And I'll call you Daddy."

I roll my eyes at her. "That shit doesn't bother me."

"What will bother you?" Her brow arches.

"Nothing bothers me."

"You're no fun."

I flash her a wolfish grin. "Stop pouting, brat, and get to the bathroom. That is, if we have a deal."

"Oh, we have a deal," she sasses as she stands from the table, "*Daddy*."

Fuck if the way she said that didn't make me hard as granite.

"Make the pictures good. Close up. I want to see everything."

She smirks, not agreeing or disagreeing. Little shit. I watch her as she prances across the restaurant, catching the eye of every motherfucker in this place. When she's been gone for five minutes, my phone buzzes.

Fuck, this girl.

She knows exactly what I like and is braver in showing me. At one time she seemed hesitant and disgusted by my ideas, but now she seems to enjoy them. The picture is of her naked pussy and asshole that's adorned with a bright blue jewel.

I'm uncomfortably hard in my slacks as I reply to her.

> **Me:** *Play with your clit but don't get yourself off. Meet me at the bar in five minutes.*
>
> **Ash:** *Your wish is my command, sugar daddy.*
>
> **Me:** *Fucking brat.*
>
> **Ash:** *Girlfriend.*
>
> **Me:** *Four minutes, little girl.*
>
> **Ash:** *Call me your girlfriend and I'll send you a picture you'll like.*
>
> **Me:** *I'll bite, my bratty girlfriend. Now show me.*

She sends a picture of two of her fingers inside her cunt. It's enough to have me stifling a groan of need.

> **Me:** *Three minutes.*

I throw money down on the table to pay the tab before striding over to an empty booth at the bar. The bartender comes over, and I order a cocktail for Ash and a beer for myself. I sense her before I see her and turn in time to see her walking toward me with a shit-eating grin on her face.

She knows she drives me insane.

It excites her.

I should be annoyed, but I'm amused at her silly smile.

"Daddy? Is that you?" she calls out, waving to me.

I can't help but laugh. She's rotten as hell. "Come sit on Daddy's lap," I say, playing along. "I missed you."

She scoots into the booth and onto my lap, rubbing against my erection with her cute ass. I grip her thighs to still her wiggly body.

"You're enjoying this too much," I growl, roaming my palm up her bare thigh. "I should have paid less."

"Too late now," she says in a triumphant tone. "You already made the deal."

No one is paying us any attention. Pity. I'd love to embarrass her for being so smug.

"Take my dick out," I rumble, "but don't get caught."

The bartender drops our drinks off. Ash takes a sip of hers and then shifts so she can sneakily slide her hand beneath her to unzip my pants. She fumbles and struggles until she manages to free my cock. Once it's out, she sits on it, rubbing against my length so I can feel how aroused she is. The fact she's still not wearing panties maddens me in the best possible way.

"You just going to rub on it or are you going to fuck it? Hmm?"

She lifts up slightly, angles her body and then slides over the crown of my cock. Slow enough to torture us both. A groan escapes her as she fully seats herself on my dick. It's always so tight when she has her butt plug in.

"Lean back," I rumble, sliding my hand beneath her dress so I can touch her clit. "Make eye contact with someone."

She curses at me, making me chuckle. "Fine. Hot suited guy, ten o'clock."

I pick up my beer with my free hand, sipping on it, as I too stare down the *hot suited* motherfucker. He must sense our attention because his lecherous eyes find my pretty girl in an instant. His eyebrows shoot up, and then he's apologizing to the guy across from him.

"You think they're gay?" I ask, pinching her clit.

"Nope. He wants me."

"Hmm."

She laughs, her pussy clenching around me. "You're jealous, boyfriend."

I'm not jealous and certainly not her boyfriend, though I bet she wishes I were. Sometimes she exhausts me with her childish nonsense. But I suppose that's the whole point of a toy—to wear a person out so that they don't obsess over the more difficult aspects of their life.

She wears me out all right. It's a good thing she entertains me and gives good head.

"His dick is probably hard," she taunts.

"You're changing the game," I warn. "I guess you don't want your fifty grand."

"I want it. You're the one who changed the game. We were supposed to do this and not draw attention to ourselves, and now you want me to make eye contact with hot guys."

"Stop calling them hot." My toy likes when I play along.

"Told you you were jealous."

"Fine. Make googly eyes with your little not-gay boyfriend over there. But do you remember the other part of the deal?"

"Where you say sweet things to me and we cuddle?"

"Before that."

I'm a spoiled boy who likes things my way too.

"You're an asshole who wants to say cruel

things."

"That's it. Can you handle it?"

"For fifty grand, I can handle anything."

I lazily rub at her clit as I inhale her hair that she pulled out of her ponytail earlier and straightened before dinner. "Your father would be mortified if he knew his precious little princess was getting fucked in a bar with everyone watching. Do you think your real daddy would call you a whore?" I nip at her ear. "That's what you are, Cinderelliott. A high-paid prostitute. You fuck me because you're so damn desperate to go to college. Nothing but a charity case. Poor little girl who tries desperately to play wicked games with a man twice her age. What is it your stepmother said? That's it... you disgust her."

She squirms and huffs, clearly hating my words, but a deal's a deal. Since she's not pulling the plug on our negotiation and forfeiting the money, I continue.

"Do your brothers take turns fucking you? Do you take all three of them at once? I bet that's why they're so fucking jealous. They've had a taste of your sweet pussy and want it all for themselves. But you're only hungry for one dick, hmm?"

"Just yours," she croaks out.

"I should pass you around to my colleagues

and brothers. If the price is right, I think you'd do anything. Money is the magical trick that has you spreading your legs. Am I right?"

"No. I only want you."

I reward her with another pinch to her clit, twisting it almost painfully for her. Her cunt squeezes my dick to the point I'm sweating with the need to come.

"I bet you'd let Keaton fuck you while our little sister watched. Is that what you want? My little brother to be inside you?"

"No, asshole," she breathes. "Just you."

This delusional girl wants things I can't give her.

Exclusivity. My undivided attention. A romantic relationship that leads to a wedding and babies.

Even though she knows we play games, I believe she often forgets the most important fact: None of it is real. None of it will ever be real. At least not with me.

"What about Perry? He'd probably give you all the sweet words in the world. Probably treat you like the princess you wish you were. But you're just a fraud. A worthless maid who wears pretty dresses bought by a rich man and fucks on his command."

"I hate you."

"You don't, because your pussy is so fucking wet, Cinderelliott. The juices running from your body feel a lot like a little girl in love with someone who can't love her back."

The *hot suited* guy is no longer trying to carry on a conversation with the person across from him. His attention is zeroed in under the table which means he can see what we're up to from his position.

"Twenty more if you let me show him what's mine." I kiss the side of her neck. "Hmm?"

"I'm not going to stop you from making me richer," she murmurs. "Do it."

I slip my hand from her clit to grip her dress and lift it. The guy's eyes bug out of his head, and he licks his lips. He says something to the guy across from him, but his attention never leaves my girl's pretty cunt. I let his peep show end by dropping her dress back down and finding her clit once more beneath the material. The guy calls a bartender over, writes something down, and hands it to him. A few seconds later, the bartender stops at our table.

"The fella over there would like to buy the lady a drink," the bartender says. "And to pass this on to her."

"He can't afford what she likes," I tell him. "Run along."

The bartender shrugs and leaves us.

"Read what your boyfriend has to say." I rub her quicker and quicker, loving the soft pants escaping her. "Now, Ash."

She picks up the business card and flips it over. "When you're finished with him for the night, call me. I can pay double, and you'll enjoy fucking someone closer to your own age a helluva lot more." She whimpers as she comes and then curses at me. "He thinks I'm a prostitute, Win."

"*My* prostitute," I say with a dark laugh.

Her body tenses at my words and guilt sluices through me, though it shouldn't since we both know the stakes here.

"Girlfriend," she growls back, squeezing her pussy like a fucking vise.

I pin the *hot suited* guy with a *fuck you, kid* glare as I come into my girlfriend or toy or paid whore or whatever the hell I feel like calling her. The point is, I let him know she's mine.

He looks away, finally understanding the message.

"Ask the bartender for some napkins, beautiful girl," I instruct, laying on the sweetness thick enough she'll get cavities. "You need to clean up all my come inside you."

It's an awkward shuffle, but she manages to slide off me once she's waved down the bartender to bring her some napkins. Her body shields anyone from seeing my dick hanging out of my pants, half-hard and dripping. Like the good girl she is, she cleans me up and puts me back to rights.

"What now?" she asks, her voice shaky.

I pull out my phone and send her seventy grand. Then, I take a picture of the guy's business card and send it to Deborah with a text telling her to find out everything she can about the guy.

"Ready, pumpkin?" I taunt, using the stupidest pet name I can come up with.

"For anything, *Daddy*."

The bad girl says it loud enough that we get several interested stares. I've definitely met my match with her.

I give her ass a squeeze as we leave, making sure to stare down *hot suited*, and soon-to-be financially ruined, guy on the way out. That'll teach that fucker to insinuate this girl is a whore—one he'd actually have access to.

Only one man gets to call her those filthy names.

Winston fucking Constantine.

CHAPTER TEN

ASH

"**D**ON'T FORGET TO tell him he's a good bird," I say, glancing over at Win in the passenger seat of the Escalade. "I'm serious."

He looks up from his phone to scoff at me. "I'm not talking to that bird."

"He'll think you don't like him."

"I *don't* like him."

"Liar."

"He's loud and smells."

"He does not smell," I growl. "Take it back."

"Maybe you should take *him* back home where he belongs."

I tense as I think about Scout getting his evil claws back on my bird. Hell no. He'd most certainly hurt Shrimp now to hurt me. I'm lucky I safely got him out of that hellhole. If only I could get myself out too.

The triplets aren't the only side of the wicked coin that's bothering me. There's the whole

Morelli situation that looms over me like a dark, menacing cloud. With each day that passes without incident, I worry about when Leo will show his face again and demand answers—answers I not only don't have but refuse to give.

"Fine, I'll tell the loud-ass bird he's precious and beautiful and the best damn bird to ever exist," he drawls out, sarcasm thick in his tone. "Happy?"

"Yep. Shrimp doesn't know they're fake words like I do." I let out a heavy sigh. "For the record, I'm not looking forward to going home."

I wince at my admission I didn't mean to slip out.

He stiffens. "You said your dad and Manda would be there."

I'd texted Dad earlier today to check in. And while he said they'd both be home, I wasn't exactly eager to get back to the place where the Terror Triplets could so easily get to me if they wanted. But I wasn't about to ask Winston to stay at his place. Despite the fun we have, in his eyes, this really is just a job he pays me for. I'm not deluded into thinking he's falling for me or anything crazy like that, though I desperately wish for it to be. One day, he'll grow tired of the games we play and move onto another willing subject, or maybe, finally settle down and marry. If I force him to house me and entertain me all hours of every day, I'll only insure he'll get bored and pretty quickly too.

The thought of him moving on to another woman sours my stomach.

"If you don't feel safe—" he starts, but I cut him off with a shake of my head.

"It's fine. Dad may be up Manda's butt, but he loves me and wouldn't let them hurt me."

He frowns at me as though he doesn't believe me, but it's the truth. If I was smart, I would confess to Dad what those monsters did to me. Truth is, though, I would die if he took Manda's side for some reason. That would be a rejection I couldn't come back from.

"I'll get you an apartment," Winston clips out, his words cold and businesslike. "There are plenty of furnished places near the office—"

"No." I let out a groan. "It's fine. I said Dad will keep me safe."

Dumb girl. Did you really think he'd beg you to move in with him?

"Don't be obtuse," he grunts out. "It makes the most sense, and you'll be safe."

"I don't want a whore's apartment, okay? I'd rather take my chances with the monsters."

My heart thunders in my chest as I wait for him to fight for me. Because a real boyfriend would do that. Someone who cared would ask me to stay and not send me to the wolves.

"Speed up," Winston says once we turn onto my road.

"What? Why?"

"Do it," he clips out.

"We're almost there. Are we not going to my house?"

"How did it feel when they were violating you? Cutting your clothes from your body? Stealing your hard-earned money? Ruining you? Hmm, pretty girl?"

His words cause a mixture of violent fury and the desire to melt at his sweet pet name.

"Horrible. I hate them," I hiss. "They're monsters."

"Then destroy what they love." His blue eyes flash in a maddened way in the darkened vehicle.

What do they love? I already know. The three matching Audis, cars that mean more to them than any other status symbol.

"This SUV can take the hit," Winston continues. "The airbags aren't going to come out. It's designed that way."

Understanding washes over me like gasoline

to my inner inferno of anger at my stepbrothers. Emboldened by his words and the fact I'm safe in this vehicle, I press onto the accelerator.

"It was an accident," he says, his voice low and commanding. "You accidentally hit the gas instead of the brake. You're so sorry."

My heart ratchets in my chest as three matching Audis parked in a row on the street come into view. As I near them, I swerve at the last minute, slamming into the back of the third one. I'm slung forward, the seatbelt bruising my chest as the crunch of metal resounds. All three of the Audis start wailing their alarms. I turn to look at Winston, my mouth gaping in shock.

I can't believe I just did that.

Holy shit.

"Back it up now," Winston instructs, guiding me on what to do. "Good girl."

I'm trembling until his palm covers my thigh, and he squeezes. Knowing he has my back does wonders to calm me. We climb out of the SUV to check out my handiwork.

All three cars are damaged. The car I hit is the worst, crumpled to the point it likely has to be totaled. The one in the middle is sandwiched between the other two. The Escalade has a broken headlight and scraped paint off the bumper, but no other visible damage.

"What the fuck?" Scout roars as he rushes from the house, his psychotic brothers on his tail.

Manda and Dad come running out next as do a few neighbors to check out the big fuss. I turn on the waterworks, bursting into tears because it's worked wonders in the past to get me out of trouble with my dad.

"I'm s-so sorry," I choke out, clinging to Winston's hand. "I accidentally hit the gas instead of the brake."

"You fucked our cars," Sully whines, gesturing to the middle vehicle. "Mine won't even be drivable."

Sparrow paces near the front car, ripping at his hair like he might cry. Scout glares at the third car that's smashed the worst and cracks his neck.

"Enough, boys," Dad barks. "Those things can be replaced. Ash cannot. Are you okay, sweetheart? Are you hurt?"

Winston gives my hand a squeeze as Dad approaches me. I let go of him to hug my dad, soaking his shirt with my tears. He pats my back and assures me everything is going to be okay and that I'm safe now. A sob escapes me, but this time it's for real.

Will it be okay?

Am I safe?

"This is an expensive mistake, Ash," Manda clips out. "Why were you even driving? You don't have a car."

I pull from Dad's embrace, taking Winston's hand again. He's cold and prickly when he wants to be, but right now, he's playing the part of supportive boyfriend. I'll definitely reward him later for this, but certainly not from my own whore's apartment. No thank you.

"Winston bought me a car," I say, smiling up at him. "He didn't think all my Uber travels were safe."

He winces at the word Uber. I nearly crack up laughing.

"At least my car seems fine," I continue. "I'd have felt awful if I totaled my new car."

"All that matters is you're safe," Winston assures me, laying it on thick. "Right?"

Manda nods as though it pains her to. Dad's is more convincing. For a split second, I see the dad I love and remember. The one who took care of me after Mom died, doing his damnedest to be both parents for me. My heart aches for what we used to have before Manda sank her claws into him.

"There's nothing we can do until morning,"

Dad says, puffing out his chest with an air of authority. "We'll call a tow service tomorrow. For now, join us for a drink, Mr. Constantine, and let me know your intentions for my daughter."

The Terror Triplets scowl my way and Manda frowns. They're not used to Dad taking the lead. Something about seeing his daughter with the richest man in the city, though, has him going into protective papa bear mode. Because I'm not a child, I don't stick my tongue out at the Mannfords. It takes every ounce of self-control, though, because I *am* petty.

"Certainly, Mr. Elliott," Winston agrees with a nod. "I think I'll take you up on that offer."

Everyone files back into the brownstone. I expect the triplets to storm off to their rooms to pout and plot revenge. Instead, they hover nearby like vultures, ready to swoop in and pick the meat from my bones. They're practically salivating for the opportunity.

Winston sits on the loveseat, pulling me down next to him. His protective arm wraps around me, holding me close. It does wonders for my erratic heart. Knowing he has my back against those monsters means the world to me. We negotiate a lot in our relationship, but this seems to come free and natural for him.

So why doesn't he let it just happen?

Why keep me at arm's length by offering to get me an apartment?

While Dad brings out a bottle of wine, I watch Manda closely. Her nostrils flare, and her dark eyes are liquid fury. But she doesn't speak out. Since my dad isn't trying to beat Winston's ass, it makes me wonder if she even told Dad about the words she discovered on my stomach. Manda doesn't seem the sort to hold back information without a purpose. Question is, what's her purpose by not telling Dad? I'd think she'd want to further drive a wedge between me and my father.

"We attended your thirty-seventh last night," Dad says to Winston, handing him a glass of red wine. "You do realize you're old enough to be her father."

The triplets glare at me, and Manda makes a disgusted sound under her breath. Winston simply chuckles. Low, dark, and evil.

"I realize this, yes," Winston throws back, his voice icy and hard. "Though, I think you have it wrong. She's my assistant and maid."

I try not to flinch at the reality of his words.

The word you're looking for is whore, Win. I'm your whore.

Dad scoffs, shaking his head, gesturing at the way Winston holds me. "And I wasn't born yesterday, Constantine. Cut the shit. We both know you're Ash's boyfriend."

I bark out a surprised laugh and sneak a look at Winston. The twitch of his jaw tells me he's entertained by my amusement, but he doesn't let anyone else know.

"If I *were* Ash's boyfriend, that would be a problem why?" Winston challenges. "She's not a little girl anymore."

Dad bristles and furrows his brow. "She just turned eighteen."

"I'm fully aware of her age, Mr. Elliott." Winston sips his wine and then nods at Scout. "There won't be any retaliation for what happened here tonight, will there?"

His words catch Dad off guard. Dad glances at me, sees my worried expression, then darts his eyes over to Scout who's practically purple with rage. He straightens and shakes his head in vehemence.

"Of course not," Dad growls, his glare pinning Scout. "The boys know it was an accident."

"See to it that they do," Winston clips out. "They seem to step in where they're not wanted when it concerns my Ash."

My Ash.

I give Winston the heart eyes as he calls it, because in moments like these hope shines through the cracks of his icy façade, contradicting all his cold words. He doesn't look at me, though I can tell he wants to, but he's in a staring contest with Dad.

"I'm not sure what you're referring to," Dad says, anger lacing his words.

"Boys, go to your rooms," Manda bites out, her tone venomous.

I'm not deluded into thinking she's angry with them. I see it for what it is. To protect her young. Scout holds my stare for a moment, unspoken promises of retaliation dancing between us, before he storms off after his brothers.

"As I said before, the boys aren't used to having a girl in the house—" Manda's words are cut off when Winston interrupts her.

"They ruined her dress and saw to it that she was unable to go to my party." Winston sips his wine. "Let's call it what it is, Dr. Mannford. Assault."

I freeze, no longer able to look at my dad. Yesterday's events come crashing down on me, making me shudder.

"They mentioned she had an issue with her

dress, but my boys didn't assault her," Manda says quickly. "Ash tends to exaggerate sometimes. Tell him, honey."

"Winston," I mutter as I glance at my dad. "It's fine. As long as they leave me alone, it's fine."

Dad's eyes narrow. Lying to him as a kid was something I couldn't do. He always saw through it. Like now. I don't even have to tell him what happened, and he knows. His jaw clenches, and then he drains his wineglass.

"Well then," Winston says, rising to his feet. "Seems like you all have it worked out. Ash, I'll see you in the morning at the office. I'll take your car home and have it brought back at dawn." He ducks down and plants a kiss on my forehead before striding to the front door.

"Let me walk you out." Dad follows him out the door and closes it shut behind them.

Silence fills the air as I wait for Manda to explode. Based on the way the vein on her forehead pulsates, I imagine it'll be soon.

"Filling that man's head with lies," she hisses. "To embarrass me—us. This won't just affect me and my sons, it'll affect your father too."

The threat has me clenching my fists. "They're not lies. The triplets are cruel to me."

"Toughen up, Ash," Manda snaps. "You'll

never make it in that man's world if you don't."

How does one toughen up against assault and threats to their reputation? She's deluded if she thinks I'll just get over what Scout and his brothers did to me. Smashing their cars feels like victory, even if I am a little sore from the impact. Completely worth it.

"I'm going to bed," I say as I rise to my feet.

Manda stands as well and walks over to me, a sneer on her perfectly made-up face. "If you can't toughen up enough to earn that spot beside a Constantine, another woman will."

I narrow my eyes at her. Surely she doesn't mean her. She's married to my dad. "You're up for that job?"

She lets out a derisive snort. "Don't be silly, Ash, I'm a married woman." She waves me off as though I'm trash. "He's better suited for Meredith Baldridge."

"Who's *also* a married woman," I throw back, remembering what I'd learned last night. Anger and jealousy race through my veins like electricity.

"But young enough to end a marriage that isn't working to seek out one that will."

With those words, she leaves me gaping after her. I may not be the best match for Winston, but I'll be damned if I let someone like Meredith

Baldridge waltz back into his life and hurt him again.

Winston belongs with someone who actually cares about him.

He belongs with me.

We may have our fucked-up games we play, but this thing between us keeps growing at an exponential rate. Soon, no matter how much he tries to deny his feelings for me, he won't be able to. I won't let him.

He can take his stupid whore apartment and shove it.

I'm not his whore.

I'm just his.

CHAPTER ELEVEN

WINSTON

I DRUM MY fingers on my desk, staring at my brother as he talks to someone on the phone. My mind is anywhere but at work. Mainly, I can't stop thinking about last night. The way the fuckwits lurked in the living room, desperate to take Ash and shred her once more. I could see the dark, overwhelming thirst in their eyes. Just waiting for me to leave so they could pounce. But, later, I'd checked in with her and she was safely locked away in her room. It drives me insane that she's unsafe in her own home and I don't have any control.

Liar.

You have all the control.

All you have to do is make that call.

The thought of demanding Ash stay with me all the time, not just when I need her, is tempting. I'd love to have her at my fingertips all hours of every day and night. I crave to devour every part of her.

But what happens when I've had enough?

The thought sours my stomach, making the coffee Deborah brought me when I walked in churn in my gut. Unfortunately, as with everything, eventually I'll grow tired of what we're doing. It'll be too difficult to end things cleanly if she's moved in with me.

Which is why giving her an apartment would be ideal. The stubborn brat, though, refuses to even acknowledge the idea. I know she'd rather me invite her to live with me, but that just isn't going to happen. End of story.

Plus, Mother would shit bricks if she knew I let my terrible maid live with me. She'd see it as weakness—because it fucking is—and do everything in her power to peel apart Ash's life. Just like she did with Meredith. But, with Meredith, she deserved to be exposed for the traitorous witch she was. Ash, however, will not fare so well if Mother gets her talons in her life, because a lot of what she would find involves me and could be especially humiliating to me and Ash.

My stomach grumbles again, and I realize I'm just hungry. I dig around in my laptop bag, fishing out the cherry gummy bears Ash bought me, shoving one into my mouth.

Perry laughs, calls Keaton a dumbass, and then shakes his head. I'm curious as to what they're talking about. It's never bothered me before that my siblings talk to each other as if they truly enjoy each other's presence. Being the eldest, I've prided myself on not needing to interact with my siblings. I thought I didn't mind, at least. Something about the way Perry smiles, happy to be talking to our brother, doesn't sit well with me. I feel as though I've missed out on something. An ache that feels much like when we lost Dad settles in my bones, making its home there.

"Enough chit-chat," I bark out, glaring at Perry.

He flips me off, ignoring me. I bite back a smirk, secretly pleased with the balls he seems to have found since he started working with me. It takes another Constantine to be effectively able to handle the top Constantine.

Ash handles you just fine.

That thought has me faltering. My mind goes back to last night when her father tried to ward me off.

"She's too soft for you."

"Ash is just a kid."

"We want her to follow her dreams and go off to

college."

I kindly—okay, so not kindly at all—told him if she was soft, she wouldn't have picked herself up after those motherfuckers ruined her dress, found a way to my party, and danced the night away like she belonged there. He tried not to let it show, but he was shocked she'd been at the party and he didn't see her. The triplets told him she had a wardrobe malfunction and wouldn't be attending the party, which he took at face value. Let's just say that after I vaguely revealed his stepsons are spawns of Satan, he wouldn't be trusting them when it comes to Ash. It's not much, but it's better than her dealing with the triplets' shit alone. At least if Baron Elliott knows what monsters his wife's kids are, especially to his own daughter, he can act like the protector he thinks he is.

The truth is, I'm the only one who can fully protect Ash.

Me.

With my money, my means, and my mother-fucking persistence.

Buzz.

Speaking of persistence…

I smile at the email on my phone from Deborah. She may have pissed me off where Perry and

Ash are concerned, forgetting her place in this company, but I'm reminded why I keep her around and pay her so well. Her ability to dig information up is invaluable.

Wes R. Hightower.

Otherwise known as *hot suited* not gay guy.

Thirty-one. Junior associate at a successful investment company, Hightower Financial Group, that his father, James Hightower, owns. It'd be a dick move to punish his father for the deeds of his son, but I think I've proven time and time again I'm a dick. I shoot a text to Harold asking him to move any and all investments that are with Hightower Financial Group. Then, I ask Deborah to see what she can learn about their clientele. Once she figures out the big spenders at Hightower Financial Group, I can make some calls. Whenever I mention moving my business or investing in something, all the other motherfuckers who want to be just like me follow suit. No questions asked. Hightower Financial Group will bleed from this monetary wound I'll no doubt inflict on their company. And when they're struggling to keep their doors open, I'll send *Wes R. Hightower* a bouquet of expensive flowers with a card that says: *You couldn't afford her before, and you certainly can't now.*

"You're so fucking evil," Perry says, as though he's inside my mind.

"Hmm?" Absently, I throw another addictive cherry gummy bear into my mouth, mildly annoyed that Ash got me hooked on this shit. For breakfast, no less.

"That face." He laughs. "It's evil. Tell me we're going to fuck up some Mannfords."

"Ash did a good job of that last night all by herself," I reveal, smirking at him.

"So I've been told," Perry says, grinning. "Keaton called to tell me he heard through some mutual friends the triplets were pissed their cars got wrecked last night. Good for Ash. After what they did…" He trails off, his features darkening and his smile wiped off his face. "It's the least of what they deserve."

I agree whole-fucking-heartedly.

"Do you think Mother knows?" Perry asks with a frown.

I throw another gummy bear into my mouth, frowning as I chew. "That Ash smashed her stepbrothers' cars?"

"No, smartass. Saturday night. That we duped her into thinking Tinsley was there all night rather than Ash."

"Why do you ask?"

He lets out a heavy sigh. "Because she called me yesterday asking me who Ash Elliott was and everything I knew about her."

For fuck's sake, here we go.

"And what did you tell her?" I lean forward over my desk, steepling my fingers.

"Just that she's a new employee here and assisting you with some things." He reaches over, stealing a handful of gummy bears from my bag. "I didn't rat out that you two were sleeping together."

I ignore his deduction about my sex life as I indulge in another gummy bear. Whatever they're made up of is a thousand times more addictive than caffeine. "Why is she concerned about Ash? How in the hell did she even get on her trail?"

"She's fucking creepy like that, Winny. You know she is. Remember that one time I wrecked one of Dad's sailboats? No one was around to tattle on me. There weren't any cameras watching when it happened. I bottomed out on some rocks and nearly drowned, but I made it out of there. I'd barely made it into the house before she was all over me demanding to know what happened. My point is, she knows shit she shouldn't before everyone else. Always."

It's true.

Mother's tentacles are deep and far reaching in this city. She's connected with the wealthy and has her fingers in the dirt too, just so she knows about every damn person that might try and threaten the Constantine name. It's part of the reason I'm so ruthless. I have my mother's blood running like ice through my veins.

"She knew about the Baldridge building," Perry throws out.

"Because Anthony told her."

"Well, it's beside the point. Someone told her about the sailboat. Someone told her about Ash Elliott."

"Speaking of the Baldridge building," I say, changing the direction of our conversation from Mother's super sleuth skills to something of importance. "I spoke to Duncan on Saturday."

"That guy is such an idiot."

"Agreed. But a loyal idiot when he feels threatened." I lean back in my chair, thinking about the phone call I received first thing when I walked through the door at seven this morning. "Apparently there were eviction notices posted on every door, even to his office. He was pissed to say the least. Now, he's bloodthirsty."

"Morelli didn't waste time," Perry marvels. "I wonder what they plan to do with that building."

"It doesn't matter. They won't have it long. I imagine Leo thought he could show his big brother how good at Monopoly he is, claiming the last piece on the board for their empire. But he forgot a very important detail."

"The Constantines own the board he's playing on?"

I flash my brother a sinister smile. "Precisely. You learn quick."

He preens at my praise, reminding me of Ash. It's nearing eight-fifteen and she's still not here. I should have negotiated something regarding her tardiness. A spanking for every minute late would have been something to look forward to. As it is, I'm just annoyed she's not here.

Those fuckfaces could have given her trouble this morning, and I wouldn't even know about it because I'm already at work.

This wouldn't happen if she lived with you…

Again, that's not happening. Ever. I can keep her safe, but that doesn't mean I have to do it under my own roof. I'm not meant to have a roommate, and I'm certainly not moving her into my bed. It'll give her the wrong idea, and as much fun as we have and as much as I want to protect her from those lunatics, moving her into my place would have her thinking something we're not.

She's my entertainment.

A sexy toy.

Expensive-as-shit whore if we're being frank.

I can keep her safe and available to me without upending my entire life to do it. An apartment near my place will have to do. Excellent security and a doorman. Someplace that allows pets so she can take her fucking bird away.

She'll have to accept it.

I won't allow her not to.

With a quick email to Deborah, I ask her to secure me an apartment for one of my employees along with my requirements and that I'll expect a set of keys in hand by the end of the day. Once that's settled and out of the way, I glance at the clock.

She's still not here.

I shoot her a text.

Me: *Your lateness makes me think your step-brothers have accosted you again. Shall I send in a white knight? I'm busy doing villain work, but Prince Perry could come to your rescue again.*

Her sassy response is immediate.

Ash: *All I heard was, "Ash, I miss you and I'm worried about you."*

Me: *You heard wrong.*

Ash: *It's okay, Win, boyfriends are allowed to worry about their girlfriends. And to answer your question, boyfriend, I'm fine. I slipped out of the house without incident, though Dad was extra attentive. Not sure what you said to him last night, but he's acting like the dad I remember before Manda tainted him.*

Me: *Blah, blah, blah… I don't care. I'm not your boyfriend. Why are you late?*

Ash: *You do care, asshole, even if you can't admit it. It's called traffic and I'm still not good at driving Bruiser. Finding a spot in the garage was a nightmare too. I'm thankful for my armored car at the moment because the orange eyesore I parked next to might door ding me when the driver goes to leave.*

Me: *You'd be doing mankind a favor if you'd take out Perry's car too. Just saying. Also, who the fuck names their car?*

Ash: *Your adorable girlfriend does.*

Me: *Stop texting and get your ass to work, maid.*

She sends me back a bunch of middle finger emojis making me laugh. Perry snorts, drawing my attention from my phone to my brother.

"What?" I demand.

"You. Just never seen you act like this before."

"Act like what?"

I know this asshole isn't about to say what I think he is. That I'm in love. Love is the farthest thing from what Ash and I have. I'd fallen victim to love once, and it nearly ended me. Meredith selfishly took my trust and crushed it beneath her size six Louboutin. I learned a great deal from that time in my life, and I'm not looking to repeat it ever again. Ash may have girlish fantasies about what this is and what we are, and my brother might be just as naïve, but I wouldn't be where I'm at today if I didn't learn to harden my heart against everyone and everything.

"In love." Predictable bastard.

"Oh, fuck right off, Perry."

He throws his head back, cracking up with laughter. "Maybe not yet, but mark my words, Ash is gonna be a Constantine one day. I'll be a cool uncle. Teach your kid sailing and shit."

"You won't teach my kid sailing and shit," I growl, my eye twitching at the idea of Perry teaching anyone how to sail.

"But you admit the hypothetical niece or nephew in this story belongs to you."

I flip him off, ignoring his taunts.

"Will he look like Ash or you? I hope Ash. She's cute. You're fucking ugly."

His taunting doesn't rile me up like he attempts to do. Instead, I send Duncan Baldridge an email to get me the details of anything he can regarding the local businesses and the Morelli's involvement. Once I've sent the email, I wave Perry off.

"Go bother Nate. I have work to do."

"Sure thing, *Daddy*," he jokes. "I wonder what colors Ash will want for the wedding."

Dumbass.

I don't reward him with a verbal response, just a roll of my eyes which has him cackling all the way out of my office.

Someone should fire his slacker ass.

CHAPTER TWELVE

ASH

I'M GRINNING AS I enter the lobby of the gorgeous building. Winston misses me and is worried about me. That shouldn't elate me as much as it does. It's not like I don't know it to be truth. He stood up for me to Manda and Dad. Bought me a freaking car. Showers me with gifts.

You worked for those, dummy.

I don't let my inner ramblings take away from my good mood. This morning, I'd been surprised to see Dad so attentive. It was like old times—before Manda and the Terror Triplets. Back when Dad and I were close as could be. His worry for me was palpable and must have been intimidating enough that the triplets didn't show their faces this morning.

I step onto the elevator, not paying attention to those around me. Someone bumps into me from behind and grabs my elbow to steady me. But they don't let go.

"Get off on the sixteenth floor and go to the women's restroom." The voice is low and deep. Familiar.

My skin crawls when I turn and meet the terrifying glare of Leo Morelli. The same man who's been haunting my dreams and has me looking over my shoulder ever since the night of Winston's birthday party. I'm disgusted I once thought him attractive. It's true, he's a gorgeous man, but the evil runs deep in his blood. I can see it in his dark eyes.

"If I don't?" I challenge, my voice a mere whisper.

"You will."

The menacing threat in his words has me obeying. I nearly stumble out of the elevator on the sixteenth floor, which appears to be a residential floor, making a beeline for the restrooms. I'm considering my options when Leo follows me inside.

"In the stall," he growls.

"What are you going to do?" I demand, holding a palm out like it might stop a grown-ass man from pouncing on me and taking what he wants.

"Not that." He laughs and points. "We're going to have a chat."

Swallowing down my fear, I step into the

handicapped stall. He pushes into the stall with me, shoving the door closed behind him and locking it. I bite back a whimper when he crowds me, forcing my back against the wall.

"Don't touch me." My glare meets his as I try and show him I'm not afraid. The tremble rippling through me gives me away.

He toys with a strand of my hair, ignoring my command. "I thought he gave up that building for you." His eyes narrow as he scrutinizes me up close. "For as pretty as you are, though, and clearly innocent, I don't think it was that simple."

"Winston's business deals are none of my concern," I throw back, straightening my spine. "Are we through here?"

"We're through when I say we're through," he snaps, the muscle in his neck bulging with his sudden bout of rage. "You see, I think he's not planning to give up that building at all. It was too easy. I fell for it because I was fixated on you being what he wanted. But, after some careful thought, I realize you're the distraction. The building is what he loves. Why, I have no fucking idea."

"You have it all figured out," I deadpan, feigning a boredom Winston would be proud of.

Leo pulls out one of the Starbursts he stole

from me. Slowly, he unwraps it and holds it up in front of me. "Lick it."

"Fuck you," I snarl, shoving at his immovable form.

He grips my jaw making me shriek. "Lick."

With tears threatening, I stick my tongue out. He makes a perverted show of rubbing the candy all over the tip of my tongue before he tosses the red square into his own mouth. His hand lets go of my face and he grins.

"Yummy," he says, his dark eyes flashing with evil intent as he chews on the candy. "Back to what I was saying before you started being a bitch." I flinch as he continues. "Find out why he's so fucking obsessed with that building. None of his family members or friends work there. It doesn't make sense."

"Maybe he just likes fucking with you," I throw back, because it seems like a Winston thing to do.

"Maybe," he agrees with a shrug, swallowing the Starburst. "Regardless, I want to know what has his dick so hard when it comes to my building. It's like he's waiting for something. All of it was too easy, and I don't buy it that he sold it to protect you. I just don't."

Gee, thanks, asshole.

"So that was the deal?" I ask, lifting a brow, channeling my inner *What Would Winston Do?* vibes. "You got to buy the building if you left me alone?"

"Seems too easy, right?"

"Seems like you reneged on your end of the deal," I spit out at him. "Accosting me and threatening me is not leaving me alone."

He barks out a surprised laugh. "Nothing gets by you, sweetheart, does it? What Winston doesn't know won't hurt him. But, if you tell him, I *will* hurt you." He steps closer, his dark eyes falling to my lips, the scent of cherry Starburst strong on his breath. "You like a little pain, though, right? From the videos I've watched many, many times, I'd say you do."

My skin heats at his words, but I refuse to let this man make me cower. "I'll try and find out why he loves that building." I'll say anything to him in order to get the hell out of the bathroom and back to safety.

"Trying isn't good enough. Find out for sure. Use your persuasive womanly abilities. It's evident you hold some kind of power over the great Winston Constantine. All I'm asking is for you to wield it." He smirks. "To help a friend."

"You're not my friend, fuckface."

"If you get me what we need, we could be. Trust me, pretty girl, you need a Morelli friend if you plan to make it in this world."

"So the Mannford triplets are your *friends*?" I demand, pinning him with a glare. "I can assure you, Morelli, I have no desire to be friends with anyone those psychopaths associate with."

He stares at me for a beat and then holds out his palm. "Give me your phone."

"You already stole the last one," I exclaim, tears pricking at my eyes. "I haven't even done anything with the new one yet!"

"Stop throwing a tantrum," he bites out, "and give me your phone. I'm adding a contact, not stealing it. When I call, you best answer. I wouldn't want to have to accidentally leak those filthy pictures of you to the press."

The thought of my indiscretions with Winston becoming front page news for all to see has bile rising in my throat. It'll ruin everything. His career, our relationships with our families, my future and college. This sort of thing is a stain on your reputation you can't erase. I hate that Leo and his minion triplets are able to hold such power over me.

I yank my phone from my purse, unlock it, and shove it against his chest. His dark chuckle chills my blood as he adds in the contact. He hands it back to me, and I notice it's my old number with the contact name: Answer Me.

"Why are you working with the triplets?" I demand as I throw my phone back into my purse. "Tell me."

He sneers at me. "The triplets are working for *me*. Not the other way around. As soon as you accept the Morellis run the show around here, the better. I'd love nothing more than to drag you into my world and show you what darkness and power really look like. Don't fucking tempt me."

I shudder at his words. The filthy, devious intent is written all over his face. I've only got eyes for one villainous bastard. The rest can go to hell.

"Why?" Despite my trembling in fear, I don't back down from my need for answers.

"Why not?" he throws back. "They want you, and I want Constantine. It seems the two of you are a package deal right now."

I sense there's more to it, but he's not offering anything up.

"Are we done?" I seethe, glowering at him.

"Find out why he wants my building, and answer my call when it comes."

"Heard you loud and clear the first time."

He studies me long enough to have me withering under his hard stare, and then he nods. "Talk soon, pretty girl."

I scramble out of the stall and the bathroom so quickly I nearly stumble over my feet. Rushing over to the elevator bank, I press on the button, hoping the doors will open soon.

"Ash?"

I whip my head to the right, surprised to see Nate striding down the hall toward me. His expression is one of suspicion.

"What are you doing on my floor?" he demands.

I can't control the shiver that rattles its way down my spine. "I, uh, accidentally got off on the wrong stop."

He narrows his eyes, glancing past me down the hallway. "Since when do you not know the floor you work on?"

"Since today," I snap back. "Jesus, Nate, I wasn't paying attention. Get off my back already."

He clenches his jaw. "Does Winston know you're *servicing* more than just him?"

"What the hell does that mean?"

I can handle Nate wrongly thinking I'm fucking someone else because Winston knows that's not true. What worries me is Nate finding out about Leo Morelli. Until I can figure out a way to get Leo off my back, I don't need Nate meddling. He already hates me. If Nate found out Leo was manipulating me into getting information on Winston, there's no telling what he'd say or do to put a wedge between us.

"We all know you're nothing more than a gold-digging plaything who happens to have grabbed my best friend's attention for a hot minute. Nothing more, Ash. Just a paid-for service."

I smack his smug face as the elevator doors open. Storming inside, I try to ignore him as I stab the button to the correct floor. He follows me inside, rubbing at his cheek.

"He may not see things clearly at the moment," Nate says, his voice low, "but I assure you, I'll make sure he does before it's all said and done. I won't let you waltz in and fuck everything up because Winston is enamored by young pussy. I'll expose you for everything you are and send your leech ass packing."

I'm sick and tired of all these assholes threatening me.

"Does Winston know you try and chase away his *young pussy* every time he turns his back?" I grin when he flinches, since I clearly hit a nerve. "Stay the fuck away from me, and don't ever threaten me again."

"Or what?" he demands. "You'll tell your sugar daddy on me?"

"That's exactly what I'll do."

He grabs my bicep. "You're the flavor of the month. I'm his friend since prep school."

"You don't warm his bed at night like I do," I hiss, yanking my arm out of his grip, "which means this *young pussy* has the upper hand and pulls rank."

Fury burns in his eyes. I'm saved by the opening of the elevator doors to our floor. I leave Nate behind, and stride through the lobby of the office, making a beeline straight for Winston's door. I could tattle like Nate suspected I would, but I'm not about to make Winston choose between a lifelong friend and me. Besides, I'm not sure I could face it if he didn't choose me like I so smugly insinuated he would if forced to. Contrary to what Nate thinks, I'm not trying to pull a fast one on Winston or get to his fortune. Sure, the money is nice, but I'm in too deep with Winston. Based on his fierce need to protect me and his damn near obsession when it comes to me, I'd like to say he feels the same. Even without the money to tether us together, we'd still be bound by an undeniable connection between us.

I have to believe that.

One thing's for sure, though.

I've had enough of bossy assholes for one day.

"You're late, Cinderelliott," Winston growls, making me smile with relief as I push through the door into his office.

I only have room for one bossy asshole. The others can all go to hell.

"Good morning to you too, boyfriend."

CHAPTER THIRTEEN

WINSTON

"**A** WORD, BIG man?" Nate darts his gaze to Ash. "Alone?"

Her brows furl, and a brief flicker of worry glitters in her eyes. She quickly schools the expression and smiles at me. "I'll go check to see if Perry needs any help."

I nod at him and check out Ash's cute ass as she exits my office. Nate closes the door behind him, hiding us from prying ears.

This should be interesting.

"Let me guess," I deadpan. "You're here to tell me I'm too close to her and you want to protect my fortune from her greedy little paws?"

His jaw clenches. "I'm that transparent, huh?"

"Indeed."

He sighs and takes a seat across from me, running his fingers through his gelled hair. It's a mannerism he's had for as long as I can remember. Dating back as far as prep school when we both played rugby. If the score was too close for comfort, he'd rake his fingers through his hair as the worry ate him alive.

Question is, why is he letting *my* life worry him to death?

"Listen," he murmurs as he studies me. "She's just not who you think she is."

I arch a brow, waiting for him to continue.

"She has secrets."

"Don't we all, Nate?"

"Hers could negatively impact you." He throws a hand in the air. "Don't look at me like that, Win. I've been your best friend for fucking forever. Sometimes, your eyes are so focused on the prize, you forget to take a look at the world around you."

"Serves me quite well, don't you think?" I challenge, coolly darting my eyes over my office, indicating all that I've achieved. "You've watched me rake in the money for Halcyon in a way my father never could. If I'm such a shrewd, focused man, how is it you'd think I'd let a little girl crawl into my world on her hands and knees and wreck everything for me?"

"I know you're not stupid. I just worry. Ever since…"

He trails off, leaving Meredith's name unspoken but no less impactful. It's because of her, though, that I know better than to let my dick and heart call the shots. The Constantine mind is what moves mountains around here.

"We've been over this. Ash is a plaything. I'm not sure why you think there's more."

"You bought her a car, a wardrobe, and fuck knows what else, man. And then I overhear Deborah arranging to have an apartment set up for an employee, which has to be her because you sure as hell never bought me an apartment. When does it end? The pussy can't be *that* good."

"The pussy is fantastic if you must know."

"Enough to put a ring on her finger?"

"What is it with you people and your obsession with marriage? I'm not marrying Ash. We've beat this horse to death."

"I'm sorry," he grumbles. "I'm overstepping, but I wouldn't be your best friend if I didn't look out for you. You've helped me out of all my fuckups over the years. Forgive me for wanting to be there for yours."

I chuckle at him. "I have the money and means to erase my fuckups, but I do appreciate your concern."

"Well, now that that's cleared up, want to go out for drinks tonight?"

Not really, but sometimes duty calls.

"Certainly. Let me just clear it with my girl-friend first." I smirk at him when his eyes widen in shock. "Oh, that's right. I don't have one. As much as Mother would love to marry me off to a rich European princess or heiress to a fortune that rivals ours, I'm not biting."

He leans in and flashes me a devilish grin. "Speaking of financially compatible matches, I heard Layla Reynard's on the market. Her husband passed away, and she inherited every-thing. Your mother would be so proud." His eyes gleam. "Not to mention, Layla never got knocked up by Reynard, so her tits and ass are still fine as fuck."

"You go from defending my honor against a poor teenager to trying to pimp me out to someone we went to prep school with and is probably still mourning the loss of her husband. Never cease to amaze me, old friend."

"Fine, maybe *I'll* hook up with Layla, because we both know Reynard was probably a terrible lay. She's probably desperate for some good dick, which I could provide. That would make Mommy Constantine proud." He winks at me. "But your mom might be so impressed she'll also want some good dick—"

"Finish that sentence and I swear to god I will strangle you with your own tie."

He laughs, and I shake my head at him. Always trying to get a rise out of me. Asshole.

"Seriously, though, man. Layla doesn't need your money. Someone like her would fit into your world. Hell, she'd probably be so happy with the security and future you'd provide that she wouldn't care about your side piece in a whore's apartment."

Ash and Nate call it a whore's apartment.

I call it protecting my investment.

"Drinks. After work. The two of us. Don't try and set me up with anyone, dickhead. Now get out of my office and actually earn your keep around here."

Satisfied and looking much less stressed on my behalf, he stands and gives me a nod. "I'll have Deborah set up a lunch through Layla's assistant. So you two can catch up. When you're swimming in more money at your wedding, you can thank me."

"I like to make it and spend it, not swim in it. Go, before I hire someone ten times more qualified than you at half the price."

He laughs all the way out of my office.

As soon as he's gone, Deborah peeks in to let

me know the apartment keys will be ready later that afternoon. Before she leaves, I make an impulsive decision.

"I'd like for you to set a lunch up for me one day soon," I say, straightening my tie and boring my stare into her. "Layla Reynard."

Her smile kicks up on one side. "Already one step ahead of you. Nate said you might be interested in meeting with her."

Meddling bastard.

"Interested might be a stretch. Necessary is more like it. That is all."

She vacates my office, and I suck in a steadying breath. Though it annoys me Nate pries and thinks he has a say over who I fuck, he's right. Ash *is* a plaything. Nothing more than a distraction from all the hard work I do. We're a transaction. I pay her, and she performs. The fucking end. There's no room in my life for love or commitment.

The only thing of value to me is my name and the stacks of endless green bills that we sit on high above everyone in the sky. It's unfortunate Ash will one day come to understand that, but it will be inevitable. As inevitable as the day Mother talks me into marrying someone of our caliber to strengthen and solidify our fortune.

As a Constantine, duty is required of me.

What I pay for behind closed doors is the reward I give myself for doing my part in this family.

"THIS IS YOURS." I walk into Perry's office where Ash is planted in a chair beside him, the two of them looking at something on his computer. "You're welcome."

Perry stares at the key on his desk, a frown of confusion marring his features. Ash, however, knows exactly what this is.

"I told you I don't want that," she snips, her neck turning splotchy red.

Her embarrassment is cute, and I'd love to exploit it if I weren't annoyed at her stubbornness.

"It doesn't matter what you want." I shove the key toward her, leaning over the desk to glower at her. "You'll take it, and you'll use it. It's yours."

"Your condo key?" Perry asks, making me wince.

"No," I clip out. "It's for an apartment. Her own apartment. So she doesn't have to worry about those douchebags retaliating for her playing bumper cars with their Audis and then telling her daddy that they're monsters."

"Smart thinking," Perry says with a nod of his head. "Those dickheads—"

"It's a whore's apartment." Her voice is shrill as she trembles with anger that's unfairly now pointed at Perry. "I thought I could at least count on you to side with me."

"He's my brother. Why in the hell would he side with you?" I pin her with a dark stare. "We're Constantines and you're—"

"The paid help. Yes, Win, you've made that abundantly clear." She stands up and starts past the desk, but I step in her way, not allowing her to throw her tantrum alone.

"Move, asshole."

"*I'm* the asshole," I growl, "for getting you an apartment to keep you safe? You're being a brat, and you know it."

She crosses her arms over her chest and glares up at me, her hazel eyes gleaming in defiance. Only Ash fucking Elliott would throw a fit over something like this. The girl will let me toss thousands of dollars at her to do dirty shit for me or buy her an armored vehicle, but a nice apartment close to her job is the threshold of what makes her a whore.

Unbelievable.

"Are we done here?" Her nostrils flare. "If so,

I'd like to leave."

Perry shifts in his seat, clearly uncomfortable at our heated discussion. I hold Ash's stare for a long minute before I give her a nod.

"We're not done discussing this, Cinderel-liott."

"Oh, Constantine, we so are." She shoves past me, her sweet scent swirling around me in her wake.

"Trouble in paradise?" Perry asks once she's gone.

"She's being unreasonable." I scoop up the key from the desk, turning it over in my palm and wondering how something so insignificant could piss her off so much.

"Not to be a master of the obvious, but you're the king of unreasonable."

I shoot him a menacing glare. "I may be your brother, but I'm still your boss."

"And yet you don't buy me an apartment." He shrugs. "All I'm saying is, Ash is more than an employee, and you know it. It's insulting to give her an apartment."

"I'm trying to keep her safe, goddammit. You saw what they did to her!" I scowl at him as I tug at the knot of my tie, needing more air to fill my lungs. "They'll do it again if given the opportunity."

"And tell me, Winny, what's the problem with the room she's got at your place?"

"It's where we play," I snap. "Not where she lives."

"So you can fuck her and buy her shit, but she can't get her mail there? That makes a whole lot of sense." He leans back in his chair, crossing his arms over his chest. "Don't fuck this up."

"There's nothing to fuck up. I pay her to please me."

"Maybe in the beginning. But now? You're an idiot if you think either of you are comfortable staying in those roles. Come on, big bro, you're not the only intelligent person around here. I can see this for what it is. She's your girlfriend whether you want to admit it or not. You basically just told said girlfriend that you want her to leave the place she's been spending all her time at to stay at an apartment you pay for."

"So?"

"In chick speak, you're practically breaking up with her."

"We're. Not. Dating."

He shakes his head, grumbling under his breath.

"What's that?" I demand, sounding oddly like

Dad in this moment.

"I said, 'If you ran Halcyon like you do your love life, we'd be bankrupt.'"

"Fuck. Off."

"Suit yourself. Ruin your life. What do I care?" He rolls his eyes. "Seriously, man, get your head out of your ass."

I toss him the keys. "You're her friend. When she's done being pissed, take her to dinner and then show her the apartment."

"And if she refuses? Want me to take her home?"

"Don't be ridiculous," I growl. "Take her to my place."

The fucker smirks, earning him the middle finger from me.

"Where will you be, Winny? Off somewhere trying to convince yourself you're not in love?"

"I'm not answering that. Just do what I say, Perry."

"Don't do anything stupid."

"That ship sailed when I hired you, a goddamn child."

"Love you too, bro."

"Fuck off."

CHAPTER FOURTEEN

ASH

MY PHONE BUZZES from my purse. I yank it out and glower at it, ready to give Winston a piece of my mind. But it's not Win.

Crap.

Asshole Stalker: *Did you find anything?*

Me: *It's been hours. What the hell do you expect me to find?*

Asshole Stalker: *Look in his emails today. See if there's anything of value there.*

Me: *He has cameras in his office.*

Asshole Stalker: *Figure something out.*

Me: *I can't! If he catches me doing a Morelli's bidding do you think he'd keep me around? Contrary to what you believe, I'm not all that important to him.*

I'm his whore.

Bitter tears sting at my eyes. I told him I didn't want the stupid apartment, and he got it anyway. He's pushing me away, and there's nothing I can do about it.

Asshole Stalker: *Follow this link.*

Dread pools in the pit of my stomach. It's a video of Winston and me. Filthy and dirty. You can't see my face very well, but there's no denying who's fucking my ass. I blink back the tears that threaten and swallow down the fear clawing up my throat.

Me: *What have you done?*

Asshole Stalker: *Nothing yet. This video is in drafts on a porn account. All I have to do is hit the publish button and then hit send on the email to one of the city's most vicious journalists. Click and click. That easy.*

Me: *You're asking for the impossible.*

Asshole Stalker: *Someone getting close to that motherfucker was impossible and you managed that with your golden teenage cunt. Put that magical pussy to work and get me something.*

There's no way in hell I'm snooping in Win's stuff and giving this asshole actual information. I'll lie. Being honest about what I can get him hasn't worked thus far.

Me: *When he's distracted on a call, I'll take his phone to the bathroom and look at the emails there.*

Asshole Stalker: *I'll expect an answer later.*

Me: *Oh no….. My phone is dying. Bye.*

I shut the phone off and attempt not to panic. He won't publish the video without getting information from me first. I have to believe that.

"Are you going to continue to pout about the inevitable?" Win's deep voice booms from the doorway of his office.

I nearly drop my phone and toss it into my purse, trying and failing to keep my features level. "I don't want to talk about this."

He strides in looking perfectly handsome and expensive and apparently completely out of reach. His features soften when he's close enough to touch. My eyes fall closed as he gently strokes his palm over my hair in what could be misconstrued as a demeaning, condescending gesture if it didn't feel so comforting. Like a kitten, I lean into his touch and sigh.

"There's my girl." Soft, sweet words from a rigid, often cruel man. "So pretty when she pouts."

I stick my tongue out, earning a chuckle from him that warms and soothes me. Sure, I'm mad at

Winston, but after my rattling text conversation with Leo, I find strength in his presence.

"I don't want the apartment. I want to stay over at your place tonight."

"Ready to negotiate?"

I pop open my eyes and meet his stare.

"You can stay the night under three conditions."

My brow arches up at his words. "I won't agree—"

He silences me with a bruising kiss. His grip finds my throat as he deepens it. When I'm dizzy and aching for more, he pulls back slightly. "You let Perry show the apartment to you and you keep the key on your chain for emergencies."

"And?"

"You suck my dick like you want to be awarded another night in my home. Make it good, and you might earn a few nights."

Determined to win this round, I rub his dick over his slacks. "Deal. But let me warn you, Constantine, I might just suck my way through the month."

"I knew there was a reason I keep you around." He smirks and moves his palm down to cup my breast. "That filthy mouth of yours, Cinderelliott. I'm quite fond of it."

And just like that, I think we've managed to drift back to familiar territory. I'm still way out of my depth with him, but he's still letting me hang on for dear life.

"I've researched some new blowjob techniques too." I grin at him in a devious way that makes him scowl. "Just wait until I stick my finger up your butt when you come. Pure magic."

"If your finger goes anywhere near my asshole, you'll be fishing those new apartment keys out of yours."

"Oooh, kinky."

"I'm leaving now," he grumbles. "Go bother Perry. He's waiting. See you at home later."

He doesn't wince at his misstep on his words, and I don't gloat. Not now. Not when everything feels so brittle and fleeting.

"Bye, Win."

✧ ✧ ✧

"I DON'T UNDERSTAND why we have to do this," I grumble, shifting uncomfortably in the passenger seat and shooting Perry an annoyed glare. "We can just go back to Winston's."

"If we did that, I'd never hear the end of it." He chuckles, turning into an apartment building garage. "Besides, it won't hurt to have someplace to go if he pisses you off."

"He always pisses me off," I throw back. "But that's kind of our thing. It's what I like about him."

He pulls into an open parking spot near the elevators and shuts off his loud car. His brows are knitted together as he studies me. "Your feelings are hurt."

"You think?"

A heavy sigh escapes him as he rubs his thumb along the leather on his steering wheel. "He's trying to do the right thing, Ash."

"By pushing me away?"

"By giving you your space. Safety. A place to call home."

Bitter tears sting at my eyes, and I busy myself with gathering up the bags of Chinese takeout we grabbed along the way. By the time I exit his orange horror show, the threat of crying has passed. We reach the elevator at the same time. He slings an arm over my shoulders and kisses the top of my head.

When I found out I was getting three step-brothers, I expected this kind of relationship. Someone who I could count on and be friends with. Someone to talk to and have my back. And when everything felt like it was falling apart, someone to hug me, putting it all back together again.

"He's just panicking," Perry says when the doors open and we step inside. "Winston's never been…" He trails off and laughs. "He's never had someone like you before."

"This apartment is case in point that he doesn't want someone like me either."

"No," he says, pressing the button for the twelfth floor. "That's not true. He wants you more than he'll ever allow his stubborn ass to admit. He's a lot like Mother. When feelings are involved, they harden to ice in an effort to protect themselves. But the person under all that coldness needs to love probably more so than either of us."

My chest aches at the way Perry speaks of his family. For as rich and untouchable as the Constantines are, they really are human at their core.

The doors open, saving us from any more conversation about Winston. I'm not sure what I expected of this whore's apartment, but I didn't expect something so normal. Winston's place is over the top expensive and new, but this place is older, restored to its original look, and probably has decades and decades of stories tucked away in its walls. I won't admit it to anyone but myself, but I can breathe a little easier in this building that reminds me so much of the one I lived in with Dad all those years after Mom died.

We walk over to unit 1200, and I hand Perry the food bags so I can fish out my keyring. After Win and I made our deal, he grabbed the keys from Perry and put them on the keyring himself. With shaking hands, I unlock the door and open it. Upon entering, I'm hit with the scent of orange and cinnamon, as if someone who lived here before liked to bake.

"This is… quaint," Perry says, taking in the small apartment with a critical, Constantine eye. "And unexpected."

The studio apartment is centered around a double bed beneath a large window overlooking more buildings. Bookcases line one wall, and a desk is on the other. There's a loveseat in one corner of the room and a coffee table. No television. Two bar stools sit beneath a small bar area that overlooks the kitchen big enough for a fridge, stove, and coffee maker. There are two doors between the loveseat and bookcase. The open one reveals a darkened bathroom.

At least my whore apartment is cute.

And quiet.

I can almost imagine myself sitting at the desk

working on my college coursework come fall.

Because Winston will be a thing of the past and you'll live here full time?

I tear my gaze from the desk and toss my purse down on the loveseat. While Perry pulls food out of the bags, I root around in the stocked kitchen looking for plates and silverware. Inside the fridge, I locate a couple of bottles of water.

"You don't have to live here," Perry says once we settle at the bar and he's heaping fried rice onto his plate. "I can go with you and look for a place you like better if you want."

"This is fine."

"Come on, Ash. Talk to me. You're too quiet."

I set my fork down and dart my eyes his way. Even though he's the younger, less put together version of Winston, he's still a Constantine. Handsome and capable. Probably normal. Some girl will be lucky to have Perry one day. If I wasn't addicted to depravity, I would go for someone like him.

Unfortunately, dark princes with fucked-up fantasies are more my thing.

"Do you think if we took away all the money and gifts and whore apartment," I say, wincing at the last part, "we'd still make it? Do you think he'd still be interested in a poor maid half his age?"

Perry laughs, boyish and loud. "You both have it so bad for each other."

"That doesn't answer my question." I elbow him. "I'm being serious."

"So am I." He shrugs and gives me a soft smile. "Winston cares about you. Not what you can do for him. Any idiot with two eyes can see that. Hell, it's why Leo Morelli tried to threaten him." I shudder at the mention of Leo, but Perry doesn't seem to notice. "You're important to my brother. Just because he's deluded himself into thinking otherwise doesn't make it any less true."

"The odds are stacked against us," I throw back. "We're not a match. Just ask Nate."

Perry's brows furl as he studies me in the penetrative way Winston has perfected. Damn these Constantines and their ability to see right inside my head. "Nate's an idiot. And you think this would be the first time Winston had the odds stacked against him and didn't come out on top?" He gives my shoulder a squeeze. "Everyone expected him to fail when Dad died. Did he? No, he came out swinging, not only growing Halcyon, but making sure every single person in this city knew he was in charge. My brother loves a challenge, and you my friend, are the most challenging woman I know."

As we finish our meal, I mull over his words. It's just an apartment. I don't have to stay here, but I do admit it gives me comfort that I have someplace to go if I ever need to. Winston is a complicated man, but he's worth knowing inside and out. He's worth fighting for, even if I have to fight him.

I'm not like that slutty princess Meredith or the other Stepford Wife wannabes in this city.

I'm Ash Elliott.

Anti-princess.

Not-so-charming villain lover.

The girl who also loves a challenge.

Win and I are an unlikely match born of filth and debauchery, but when you dust us off, we shine up nicely.

Perry finishes up his food and starts to clean up. I'm still thinking over our conversation when my phone buzzes. I'd turned it back on earlier, and I'm not surprised to find a text from Leo.

Asshole Stalker: *Well?*

Me: *There's a lot of emails about the building you bought.*

Lies.

Asshole Stalker: *To who? What did they say?*

Me: *Some chick named Meredith.*

I'm going to hell for that one.

Asshole Stalker: *Are they going to try and get it back?*

Me: *It's Winston. What do you think?*

I'm lying through my teeth while trying to make it sound legitimate. Leo is calculating and terrifying. Not sure if he'll buy it. If he asks for proof, I'm shit out of luck.

Asshole Stalker: *You just bought yourself another few days of anonymity. Keep up the good work, snitch.*

I want to send him a thousand middle finger emojis but settle for three.

"Winston?" Perry asks, making me nearly jump out of my skin. "He's the only one you grin so evilly for."

I shove my phone into my purse and shake my head. "Just some asshole who thinks he can tell me what to do. I miss Shrimp. You ready to go already? The whore apartment is skeeving me out."

He laughs, and I let out a sigh. I've dodged the first Morelli bullet. Let's just hope I can dodge the rest.

CHAPTER FIFTEEN

WINSTON

THANK FUCK IT'S Friday. This week has rushed by in a blur as I've put out one fire after another. It's like the universe is taunting me. Luckily, Ash is more than a pretty face. Pretty competent too. Between her and Perry, they equal the ability of any mid-level associate, which is surprising considering how green they both are. I've had them both running in a million different directions for me. Perry will make it on his last name alone, but it does comfort me knowing Ash plans to go to college. She'll be successful one day, that's for damn sure. After our fight over the apartment earlier this week, things have slipped back to the way they were. She works hard every night to please me, and I reward her by not sending her away.

I'm such a dick.

Ash doesn't seem to be complaining, though.

As if she's been summoned by my thoughts

alone, she walks through my doorway, a paper in her hand. "Perry asked me to give this to you. It's a list of businesses in a one-mile radius of the Baldridge building."

I've been too busy to do much digging, and Duncan has been useless in getting me information. But, as much as I want to scour the list, my attention is stuck on Ash. Today, she looks hot as fucking sin in a classic cut, navy-blue and white polka-dotted dress that fits all her curves in a tasteful way. It's very 1950s but fuck if I don't think it's the hottest thing I've ever seen.

"Close the door," I rumble, "but don't lock it."

Her brow lifts in surprise, but she doesn't argue. Instead, she swivels, her dress swishing around her, and obeys. I roam my stare up her shapely calves, ass, and hips, appreciating each part of her body. Once we're sealed in the privacy of my office, I tug at the knot on my tie, loosening it so I can breathe.

"You've been too busy to even take me to lunch this week," she says as she saunters over to me and sets the paper down on my desk. "I was beginning to think my boyfriend was losing interest."

Not losing interest.

Trying to use my brain instead of my dick.

Yesterday's lunch was spent with Layla Reynard. What I thought would be a good opportunity for me to put distance between me and Ash, reminding me of what I'm supposed to be interested in, turned out to be a torturous encounter.

Layla was beautiful, just like Nate claimed. Rich, polite, a perfect trophy.

But she wasn't Ash.

Nothing about her sparked my insane need to possess and own and devour.

Rather than calming my tumultuous mind, it only sent it spinning further into chaos. I'd come back from that lunch and fucked Ash so hard over my desk I'm pretty sure the entire building heard her unravel with my name on her lips.

"Not your boyfriend," I murmur, though I don't put much of a punch into my words. "And I pay too much not to see my investment pay off."

She rolls her eyes as though she's used to my taunting, but I notice it hits her the wrong way based on the way she winces. "Whatever."

"Do you like working here?"

A genuine smile touches her lips. "I do. It's exciting. Lots to do. I'm better suited for working here than dusting your immaculate condo."

Plus, she earns a paycheck that more than pays for the rent on her "whore" apartment as she calls it—the one she's only stepped foot into once.

"Let's be real, you only pretend to dust."

"At least here I don't have to pretend." She cocks her head to the side, studying me. "I can see the cogs turning in your head. You have a nefarious plan. One that involves me. Oh god, I hope it pays well."

I smirk at her smartass teasing. "You know everything I do pays well. Still planning to go to college in the fall?"

She tenses and frowns. "What happens between us doesn't change that, Win. I had plans before I met you, and those won't suddenly disappear now that you're my boyfriend."

"Not your boyfriend, and someone's a tad defensive."

"You *are* my boyfriend and I'm not. Just don't want you thinking I'm a freeloader is all." She shifts her gaze to the windows behind me, not meeting my stare. Whoever is filling her head with nonsense will get their ass chewed out later. My guess it's either Deborah or Nate since those two are the only ones who seem to have a problem with Ash this week.

"It's not freeloading when you work for it,

Cinderelliott. We both know you make enough to pay for your own apartment, but your spoiled ass refuses to live in it."

"It's too small for Shrimp to fly around. Besides, I'd rather just bug you all night." Her body relaxes and she arches a brow in question. "So what are we doing today?"

I lean back in my chair, flashing her a wolfish grin. "You."

"Duh," she sasses. "I need more details before I agree. What am I working for?"

"How about your entire first year tuition paid in full?"

She gapes at me. "Winston, that's too much. It's like—"

"Right at seventy-five grand. Yes, I know. And it's not too much. You'll see."

"I won't traipse around the office naked. Deborah already hates me enough." She crosses her arms over her chest, daring me to argue. At least I know who's been making her feel like shit. Something I'll deal with later.

"It's like you don't even know me," I tease. "You know my imagination is far more colorful than that."

"Unfortunately."

I chuckle and gesture to her purse sitting on

the bookshelf. "Get your phone."

She prances over to her purse and fishes it out. "You can film it from your phone. It doesn't always have to be from mine."

"Who said anything about filming? You really are a filthy girl."

She pretends to paint on lipstick with her middle finger. "Name your terms, Constantine."

"I will have Harold open a college fund for you in the amount of seventy-five thousand that can only be used for tuition and anything related to your education. No one can access the funds. Not me. Not your father. Not your stepmother or stepbrothers. Hell, not even you. At least not without proof of where the money is going."

"You don't trust me to spend it on school?" Hurt shines in her hazel eyes.

"I don't trust you not to spend all of it on sweet words from me." I smirk at her. "I just like the idea of the money being there and untouchable no matter what happens."

Uncertainty dances across her features.

"Don't worry, little girl, you can pretend to be my girlfriend some more. I haven't gotten bored of you yet."

She rolls her eyes. "You're an asshole."

"I think you meant to say, 'You're an asshole,

boyfriend.'"

"Nah, I don't want to call you that if you want it."

"Maybe I should pay you to say it."

"And then my reverse psychology will have won," she teases with a laugh. "I'll have outsmarted the great Winston Constantine."

"You wish it were that easy." I gesture at her phone. "FaceTime your dad. Have a little chat. Let him know your boss paid your tuition for the first year."

"Sounds too easy."

"Because I'm not done."

She glowers at me. "Of course not."

"Make the call while sitting on my desk."

"Fine, but you owe me dinner tonight. Someplace romantic." She grins at me in that innocent but still deviant way of hers. "*Boyfriend.*"

I foolishly play her games because she's always down to get dirty with my own fantasies. But, where I can turn off the good sex and easy banter with the snap of my fingers, Ash will still be staring at me with goddamn hearts in her eyes. It's a mistake to lead her on, but I can't stop. She's an addiction—one that when I quit cold turkey, will destroy us both.

"That's a whole other negotiation. We'll discuss dinner later. Right now, I want your panties in your purse and your bare ass on my desk." I pat the smooth surface. "I don't have all day, woman."

"I want steak, and we need to go by the candy store again," she grumbles, shimmying out of her panties while hiding all the good parts from my viewing pleasure as though she won't be spread out like a fucking Thanksgiving feast in a few minutes. "You're out of gummy bears."

My mouth waters at the mention of them. She's created a monster. All my teeth are going to rot and fall out if I keep eating that addictive, chewy-ass shit.

With a victorious grin, she struts over to me. I roll back to give her space. She sits on the edge of the desk, spreading her thighs and pulling her dress up to expose herself as I slide my chair back closer.

"Scoot your ass to the edge," I instruct as she settles her heels on the arms of my chair.

"I feel like I'm at the gynecologist."

"Does your gyno lick your needy pussy?"

"Ew. Don't be sick, Win."

I give her pussy a playful smack. "Too late. Already sick. Now get him on the phone."

"Are you going to just stare at it and admire it

or are you going to lick it?"

"I'm not licking anything until you get your daddy on the phone, little girl. I want to make you whimper and moan as you tell him your sugar daddy took care of you when he couldn't."

"That's mean."

"Marrying that wicked witch with her rotten turds and treating you like you weren't the most important thing in his world was mean," I snap, a little too testily.

Her brows crash together, all playfulness gone. "Just when I think my boyfriend doesn't care, he says something super romantic to me."

"Get your head checked if you found anything about that statement remotely romantic."

"We've ascertained I'm not quite right up here," she sasses, "but I totally blame you."

I give her pussy another slap that has her scowling at me. Finally, she dials her father. As soon as she starts to chat it up with him, I run my tongue along her slit, reveling in the sharp hiss of air she sucks in. She groans as I slip a finger inside of her while simultaneously sucking on her small clit. Her body is slick inside, clenching around my finger like she wishes it were my dick. I rub at her g-spot, thrilled when she whimpers.

"Are you okay, honey?" her dad asks, making

me smile against her pussy.

"Great. Just sore from my run this morning."

Big liar. The only thing she runs is her mouth.

They continue to chat, but she doesn't bring up the tuition. I pull away, giving her a look that demands she moves the conversation along. She grimaces, but then whimpers again when I go back to driving her wild.

"I, uh, wanted to tell you the uh, unhhh…"

"The what?" her dad asks. "Honey, are you sure you're okay?"

"Yes," she cries out. "I'm fabulous. Very happy." She gasps. "I'm just so thrilled that Winston is paying f-for my first year of school."

Silence aside from the sloppy sounds of my mouth on her pussy.

"Manda said she would be paying for your tuition." His voice is strained and a bit angry. "We don't need Mr. Constantine to step in."

"I don't mind it at all," I say, and then nip at her clit. "It's my pleasure."

"I didn't realize he was listening in," Baron grumbles. "Maybe we should discuss this later."

"There's nothing to discuss, Dad. Win and I made a deal."

"What sort of deal?" he demands.

"Just work stuff." She trembles, her ass lifting

off the desk, desperately seeking my tongue. "We worked it all out."

I suck on her clit and then pop off loudly, never losing stride as I finger her g-spot. "The money will be in an account that can't be touched. By anyone."

I let those words sink in, pleased that I've rendered him speechless. My focus is on Ash's face that she manages to keep impassive aside from the gnawing of her bottom lip between her teeth. The moment she comes, she whines and clamps her eyes shut, her pussy milking my finger like it'll come inside her needy little hole.

"Don't cry, honey," Baron says. "You know I'm sorry about your college fund." He curses and sighs. "Look, I have to get back to work. We'll discuss this later. I love you."

"Love you too, Dad."

She hangs up and glowers at me. "Happy?"

I slide my finger out of her and give her pussy another smack. "Unbelievably so."

"You're such an asshole."

We have a stare down as my dick hardens with the need to fuck her sassy mouth. I'm about to suggest it when someone knocks.

"What?" I bark out.

"You have an important visitor," Deborah

calls through the door.

Ash scrambles off the desk and quickly yanks her dress down to cover herself. My fingers are still wet and the office smells like her sweet pussy.

"Send them in," I say, enjoying Ash's annoyed growl.

When the door opens, the blood that had been making my dick throb turns ice cold.

Fuck.

CHAPTER SIXTEEN

ASH

OH MY GOD.

Caroline Constantine. A golden, older replica of the man beside me. His freaking mother. I imagined a million different scenarios of when we'd meet, all including me making a wonderful first impression. Not this. Not walking in after the wicked act that transpired between me and Winston. A mother knows things. This one, I bet, doesn't miss a thing.

It makes me feel dirty. Less like a girlfriend and more like a prostitute. I just let him eat me out in exchange for my college tuition. I'm ready to run away to my whore apartment and hide forever if we're being honest.

Winston clears his throat, seemingly rattled by the intrusion. If he's rattled, I'm completely fucked. It normally takes a lot to rattle him.

Caroline's icy glare sweeps over me, slowly cataloging every detail from my flushed cheeks to

the phone in my hand to the way I shift awkwardly on my heels. The room smells like sex, which
makes me cringe in horror.

"Mother," he grunts out, finding his voice.
"This is my assistant, Ash Elliott."

Right. Assistant.

Not girlfriend.

It's a painful sting of reality.

"I know who she is." Caroline waves a dismissive hand at me. "I need a word with my son."
She gives me a fake-as-hell smile. "Alone."

I glance at Winston, but he won't look at me.
He's gone rigid. So much for saving me from the
evil queen. I try not to wither under her hateful
glare.

"I'll, uh, just see if Perry needs anything," I
stammer as I turn and start for the door.

"I'm sure Perry can handle himself just fine."
The warning in her voice has me shrinking away
from her. "Perhaps you should…" She waves
another manicured hand at me. "Freshen up in
the ladies' room."

My cheeks burn hot. All I can do is nod before I bolt out of Winston's office. His secretary,
Deborah, smirks at me, clearly enjoying my
embarrassment. Rather than let her see me
frazzled, I do as Caroline suggested and freshen

up—and put my damn panties back on.

The way Caroline had looked at me still haunts my mind. As though someone like me will never be good enough for her son. Sometimes I wish I'd met Winston four years from now—after college. So that I'd have my own value. That money wouldn't be the connecting factor. That he'd see me as a successful woman with similar bedroom tastes.

But I'd never have had the opportunity to meet him had things not transpired the way they did.

With a sigh, I head over to Perry's office, hurrying past Nate's so I don't have another confrontation with him like earlier in the week. He stops tapping away on the computer to smile at me as I enter.

"Hey, sis," he greets, his blue eyes twinkling with mischief.

I shake my head at him. "Don't let Winston hear that. Or Nate for that matter. He already thinks I'm trying to get Winston to put a ring on me."

Among other things. Like fucking someone behind Winston's back.

If only that were the worst of my worries. But, on top of everything, I have this building, burning worry about what I'll do about Leo. I haven't heard from him in a couple of days, ever since I fed him false information, which should bring relief, but it only brings uneasiness. It won't be long before he accosts me again to see what I know. I've been lucky to come out unscathed thus far, however, I'm not sure that will always be the case.

Perry's features grow serious. "Nate giving you shit?"

"Just protecting his friend." I let out a harsh breath. "We have bigger problems."

Besides Leo and Nate and the triplets and all the other crap in my world.

"Oh?"

"Your mom…" I trail off and wince. "Let's just say I met her for the first time, and it didn't go well."

"She's here?" He sits up in his chair, frowning. "Why?"

"I'm not sure, but she ran me out of Winston's office."

He sighs and pinches the bridge of his nose. "It'll be fine. She's just… overprotective sometimes." His blue eyes find mine. "Speaking of overprotective, have the triplets fucked with you anymore since the night of the party? You've seemed edgy this week."

It warms my heart that Perry seems to care about me and my wellbeing. Where Winston tries to pretend he doesn't, Perry makes it clear he does care. I'm glad we've become friends. Since the triplets ran all mine off, it's nice to have someone to talk to—someone who isn't interested in getting me naked.

"No," I tell him with a shrug. "But, in their world, that's scarier. If they're quiet, then they're up to something." Just like with Leo. Of course, I don't mention that.

"Hmm," Perry says, an evil smirk on his face that reminds me a lot of his wicked older brother.

"You know, when Win does that, he's up to no good."

"I'm a Constantine, Ash. We're never up to any good."

AFTER HELPING PERRY for a few hours until five, I leave his office to seek out Winston. His office door is still closed. I'm dying to know what his mother said. I walk over to his office and knock.

Deborah ends a call and clears her throat. "Mr. Constantine has left for the day, miss."

Miss.

As though I'm some random visitor.

Deborah knows I'm way more than just a visitor for Winston, and yet she seems to get a thrill by treating me as though I'm nothing to him.

"He went to dinner with his mother," she reveals, forcing a fake smile. "Could I leave him a message?"

I grit my teeth and shake my head. "Nah, I'll see him at his place later."

It's a lie, but I enjoy seeing her bristle. Truth is, I don't know if Winston plans on seeing me later. He's never cut off contact from me like this or not given me some sort of itinerary. I feel sort of abandoned, but I certainly don't let her see that.

He gave you an apartment.

My blood boils at that thought, but it's another sick dose of reality. Am I reading into what we have more than I should?

No.

He's just being a stubborn idiot.

"Of course," she clips out. "If you'll excuse me, I have work to do."

I gather up my things and am heading out when my phone buzzes with a text from Winston.

Win: *Wait for me at my place tonight.*

Me: *I might be busy.*

Win: *Don't fish for attention. I promise to shower you with attention and come later.*

He can be so gross, and yet I still smile like a lovestruck idiot.

Me: *On a scale of one to ten, how much does your mother hate me?*

Win: *It doesn't matter how she feels, Ash.*

His words are serious and kind of sweet. Because we need levity, I send him a bunch of heart eye emojis that earn me several middle fingers.

We're okay.

Whatever she said to him or says to him will glance off him, not affecting things—us. I'm relieved because though this is a big game with a lot of money involved between the two of us, it's a game I'm not done playing. A game I've become incredibly invested in. A game where I want us both to win.

"WHEN'S DADDY COMING home?" I ask Shrimp, running my finger along the top of his pink head. "We're bored, huh?"

Shrimp sings and flutters his wings. Cutest little bird ever. I sigh, glancing at the time on my phone. I've been waiting at Winston's place for a couple of hours, and he's still not here.

Someone knocks on the door, startling Shrimp. He flies up to the artsy light fixture in the living room, chirping at me as though I scared him on purpose. I laugh as I stand and make my way over to the door. Just as I peek through the hole, I see Nate on the other side pulling out his keys to unlock it. I pull it open and give him a bitchy smile.

"He's not here. Sorry."

He rolls his eyes, walking into the condo anyway. "I can wait."

Sighing heavily, not even bothering to be polite, I shut the door and follow him. Just like last time, he makes himself at home, pouring himself a drink. But rather than letting him be, I walk over to him, crossing my arms and glaring at him.

"If you're trying to intimidate me, it won't work," I spit out.

Shrimp flaps his wings but otherwise remains quiet. He doesn't like when I get upset.

"I'm not trying to do anything," Nate grumbles and then drains his liquor in one gulp. "I'm waiting for Winston to discuss some business with him."

"Then you'll have to deal with me for a while. I'm not sure when he's returning."

He meets my stare with narrowed eyes before setting down the empty glass on a small table. "I'll deal with you then." His nostrils flare and then he gestures upstairs with a lift of his chin. "Need to take a piss. Maybe you should pour us both a drink."

Ignoring him, I suck in a calming breath as soon as he's disappeared up the stairs. Shrimp chirps at me but won't come back down. "I know, I know. He's an asshole," I tell my bird who's a great judge of character. "But he's Winston's best friend."

A short while later, he returns and helps himself to another drink. I scroll through my phone, pretending as though I have a life and am sucked into social media. In reality, I watch Nate from the corner of my eye as he watches me.

"When are you going to realize you're just a toy for Winston?" he asks, sipping his liquor. "All rich boys grow tired of their toys eventually. Hell, based on the fact he's elsewhere and you're here, entertaining me, I'd say maybe it's already happened, but you're just too naïve to see it."

I flip him off, not rewarding him with an answer. He chuckles and then calls to my bird—

here, birdie birdie—like he's a puppy. Shrimp flaps his wings hard, the equivalent of a birdie *fuck you*. I bite back a smirk. Nate looks at his watch and then downs the rest of his drink.

"As much as I'd love to spend all night waiting on Winston, I have a date to get to." He sets his glass down and walks past me. "I'd say see you soon, but I'm not sure that'll be the case. Hell, I may never see you again. I'm sure you were fun while it lasted." He pauses to shoot me a triumphant grin. "Perhaps you should ask him how lunch went with Layla yesterday. I heard Caroline was hoping he'd ask her out. You know, since she's not a poor, money-hungry maid and comes with her own fortune."

Layla?

Lunch?

I keep my features cool, but hurt slashes at my heart, quick and gutting. Winston never mentioned lunch with anyone.

Why would he?

He's not your boyfriend. He's only been trying to tell you this since day one, idiot.

Oh. My. God.

I'm seriously deluding myself, aren't I?

Satisfied with my silence, Nate leaves without another word, the door closing with a loud bang after him. Shrimp starts chirping at me as though to bitch me out for even having a conversation with Nate. To take my mind of his words and to wait for Winston, I take a long bath. Nate's words continue to dig under my skin, though, and get inside my bones.

Maybe this lunch thing was just that. Lunch. But what if it wasn't? What if he's getting bored with me?

Or worse yet, when his mother and his best friend finally convince him I'm just a plaything and he lets me go to set off for a more appropriate match like this Layla woman?

We started this out as a negotiation—me indulging his insane kinks for cold, hard cash—but it evolved into something deeper for me. Sure, we joke a lot about him being my boyfriend, but a giant part of me wishes he was. Aside from his freak nature, Winston is a catch. He's successful and confident and gorgeous and protective. I like him. Really, really like him. Somehow, I think he really likes me too. So why does it all feel so brittle and fleeting?

Because it is.

The apartment was the first attempt to keep you at arm's length. Who knows what his dinner with his mother will bring?

At the sound of the front door opening, I dry off and throw on a robe. I'm just rounding the corner to see Winston walking in. Shrimp sings a happy song to him before divebombing him and landing on his shoulder. I expect him to swat the bird away. Instead, he strokes him gently with his thumb and speaks lowly to him. My heart does a twist inside my chest, making me realize Winston Constantine is capable of breaking me if he wants to. Being so vulnerable to such a powerful man is unnerving.

"How was dinner with your mother?" I clip out in greeting, my tone laced with hurt and accusation. I immediately hate myself for being so transparent.

Winston turns to regard me, his features impassive and cool. The only tell of his interest in me is the slight flaring of his nostrils and heated flicker in his blue eyes as he skims his gaze over my bare legs. Something catches his eye, and his brows furrow.

"Who was here?" he asks, gesturing to the empty glass on the table.

Shrimp flies over to his cage and noisily starts pecking at his food.

"Your bestie," I state a little testily. His brow arches and I clarify, "Nate."

For a beat, all Winston does is stare at me. It reminds me of the cold, unfeeling way his mother looked at me. I suppress a shiver and instead lift my chin. Whatever transpired between him and his mother has been brought home with him. He's clearly irritated and frustrated, hardening those emotions with his indifference he wears like metal armor.

"And what did my bestie want?"

I huff and shrug. "To use your prissy warm towels." And to make me feel like shit.

His eyes narrow as he studies me. All that can be heard is Shrimp's pecking. My heart thunders in my chest as I wonder if this'll be the moment he tells me to leave. That he let his mother whisper in his ear and tell him I'm not good enough for her eldest Constantine son. That maybe Nate was right and he wants to see this other woman. The silence drags out between us, neither of us budging or speaking.

It'll be fine.

Whatever happens will be okay.

I earned that first year of tuition fair and square in his office earlier today. And if there's something I know about Winston, it's that he always follows through on a deal. At the very least, I had some fun and have school taken care of for a bit.

So why does my chest ache?

Because you don't want this to be over. Because it's not just about money for you.

"Cinderelliott?" He tugs at the knot of his tie. "How would you like to earn some money?"

The familiarity of our game has relief flooding through me like a rushing river.

This isn't over.

We're both in too deep to walk away now.

I just need to convince him if you take all of the money and tuition and gifts away, we're still worth something.

I have to. I will.

CHAPTER SEVENTEEN
WINSTON

THE AIR IS charged with *something*. A mixture of my anger and Ash's defiance. I'd walked into my condo, ready to send her home—for good—but as soon as I saw her, everything changed.

Again.

Seems she has a way of doing that to me.

My thoughts drift back to dinner with Mother, hardening my heart to the woman before me.

✧   ✧   ✧

"DO YOU EVEN really know her?" Mother asks, her voice slightly condescending as though she's chiding a child for his innocent take on the world.

"I know enough."

"Enough." Mother sips her wine, taking her time before speaking again. *"That's vague and leads me to believe you know nothing at all."*

Irritation burns in my gut. "She's my maid and

assistant."

"Who lives with you." Her blue eyes narrow, pinning me in place. "When were you going to tell me?"

"She doesn't live with me," I grind out, anger surging through me. "She has her own apartment."

"Not what Nate says."

Silence fills the air as I study my mother. Beautiful enough to grace magazine covers or be shown on the big screen, but evil enough to destroy empires with her icy glare alone.

"I wasn't aware you and Nate have conversations about me behind my back."

"There's a lot you're not aware of, Son. Is it because you're letting a little girl distract you from your place in this family?"

I pick up my glass and drain my wine before setting it down with a hard clink. "Enough of the games. What do you want?"

"Games? Your future is anything but a game."

I scrub my palm over my face and let out a sigh. "I had lunch with Layla Reynard."

"I heard."

"I figured you'd be thrilled." I cock my head to the side. "That is, unless you've got plans for me and Meredith."

She smirks. "Oh, Son, indeed I do have plans for Meredith."

I wait for her to elaborate but, naturally, she leaves me hanging. I'm tired of her meddling so I wait her out, eating my filet without speaking a word. When I'm finished, she finally says something.

"Have you ever asked the Elliot girl how her mother died?"

"No, because she's not what you think she is to me."

Keep lying to yourself and everyone else, Winston.

"Hmm." The waiter refills our wine, and the silence is broken again by Mother. "I would hope that you, of all people, would see that when you consort with people beneath you, they will drag you down on their way up."

Ash isn't like that, but I'm not about to argue the point with her.

"It's times like these, I see that eighteen-year-old young man. So naïve to the world we live in." She pauses letting her insult sink in. "She'll use you. Just like Meredith tried to." Another beat of silence. "She's just a plaything, Son, and you're too old to be playing with toys."

Her words hit me right in the chest. I know what she says makes sense, but hearing it outside of my head and from another Constantine—not just Nate—has it sticking in my brain. Ash needs money. I have it. We trade sex and games for it. The end.

It's nothing more than that; and can never be more than that. Because if I somehow let myself think otherwise, the matriarch of the Constantine family would swoop in, talons bared, and shred Ash to bits.

It's better this way.

ALL OF MOTHER'S lecturing, while it had gotten to me at dinner and had me seeing reason where Ash was concerned, was forgotten in the blink of an eye. The second I saw Ash looking young and beautiful and sassy in nothing but a robe, I forgot everything. All I wanted to do was rip off the offending clothes and push her to her knees.

As much as I want to fuck her one last time, because soon it'll have to be the last time, there are more pressing things to discover. Like why Nate was hanging out with Ash while I wasn't here. And how she's unperturbed as though it's a normal thing for them or that it wouldn't bother me.

She'll use you. Just like Meredith tried to.

Mother's words echo inside my head over and over again.

"Name your terms," Ash says, approaching me slowly as though I'm a wounded animal that might bite.

I'll bite all right.

But I'm not wounded.

I'm the wounder.

I run my tongue along my bottom lip, my mouth watering to taste her. She's every bit as addictive as those goddamn red gummy bears. I want to devour her. Over and over again. She's hooked me just as she did with the ridiculous candy made of god only knows what. If I keep her, she'll do harm in the long run. Just like the damn sugary bears. A fucking cavity. That's all she is to me. A fleck of dirt in my otherwise pristine world, burrowing deeper and deeper with every passing moment. If I don't do something about it soon, she'll hit a nerve.

She smirks.

Fuck, she's already hit a nerve.

The kind that I keep hidden and well preserved.

A rush of pleasure, not unlike how the sweet treats affect me when I eat one, slides through my veins, heading south. My cock stiffens in my slacks, eager to play with my dirty maid.

She's just a plaything, Son, and you're too old to be playing with toys.

Again, Mother's words mock me.

It's a good reminder, though. If my mother

believes her eldest son is in danger—again—from a female dead set on ruining him, she'll do what every mama bear will do: claw poor little Ash out of my life until she's nothing but shreds. Unlike Meredith who had protection of family and her family's old money, Ash has nothing. Caroline Constantine will feast on the bones of her life and when she finishes, there'll be nothing left. Ash wouldn't emotionally or financially recover from a Constantine war.

Which is another reason why I need to end things.

Soon.

The longer I hold onto this decadent current that flows between Ash and me, the more at risk the both of us are. I'm at risk of forgetting I have a brain and accidentally using my heart which has proven unreliable in the past. Ash is at risk of drowning in everything wicked and awful that is me.

She has her education fund set up, something I got Harold started on right after Mother came to visit the office this afternoon. Ash can go to school in the fall, and no one can stop her. Not her stepbrothers or stepmother. Not her father. Not the Constantines.

Tonight, this all ends.

It has to.

She may not want the "whore apartment" as she calls it, but it's beyond necessary. It'll keep her safe from those fuckwits and me safe from making a terrible decision… like keeping her.

"Win," she murmurs, her brows crashing together. "You're trembling."

I steady the slight shake of my hands by curling them into fists. Breathing in her sweet cherry scent has my mind racing at all the things I still want to do to her—all the things I won't be able to after tonight.

"Five grand," I clip out, my voice even and icy. "For every cruel insult you can take."

If I'm going to toss her back into the world, at least she won't have to rely on anyone but herself. I'll send her out into it with a padded bank account.

She scoffs. "It's like I've won the lottery. We both know I can handle your cruelty."

It's on the tip of my tongue to tell her that after we fuck, she can pack up her shit, including her noisy-ass bird, and leave. But then she's crowding me, her small hands roaming up my chest.

"I'll up the ante." The soft purr of her voice is like the vibration of music in a dance club. It infects my every molecule with the music. Pulses through me. Finds a way inside my mind and my soul. "It'll cost ten grand for each insult."

"If?" I raise a brow at her.

"You're learning, Mr. Constantine." She smirks. "If you deliver a little physical pain along with it. I want to feel the sting of your hand or your belt or your teeth so that it matches how your words feel."

Fuck, I'll miss this. Her body, her words, her ability to challenge me.

"You can't handle that level of… me."

"I can handle you at any level, Win, and you know it. Do we have a deal or no deal?"

Her hazel eyes burn into me. So fucking beautiful. In another life, I could be someone like Perry. Someone who wouldn't give a fuck about his last name or his mother. Someone who might allow himself to fall for a girl like Ash Elliott. To be a prince and marry a princess. Have a house full of strong-willed but no doubt beautiful children. Live happily ever after. The whole fairytale shebang.

But I'm not the prince.

Ash is just the maid and not a princess.

I'm the villain and my story doesn't end with a carriage ride into the sunset.

It ends with a girl in tears taking her cherry Starburst scent and fucked-up proclivities that match mine and her loud-ass bird out of my life. For good. Because that's the only way the maid gets her happy ending.

"A million tacked on if when we're done fucking, you go home to Daddy." I pin her with a firm glare. "That'll take care of undergraduate and grad school both. Take it or leave it, filthy princess."

Her nostrils flare, and her cheeks turn pink as I wait for her to accept the terms. She darts her tongue out and licks her lips, her head shaking in vehemence. "No."

"It's a million dollars, Cinderelliott. The answer is never no when a million dollars are involved."

"I'm not going home tonight." She lifts her chin and pins me with a firm stare. "I don't want your million dollars handed over just like that. I want to earn it. One cruel, incredibly expensive word at a time."

Poor girl. She thinks I mean only for tonight. I need her gone tonight and forever. It's the only way.

"Suit yourself," I growl, tugging at the tie on her robe. "How will I know when you've had enough?"

"Like a safe word? I don't need one."

"Your tears and begging won't be enough, because we both know you secretly like it. How will I know I've pushed you past what even you are comfortable with?"

Her brows lift in surprise. "Big plans in the bedroom tonight?"

"It's the grand finale. Must go out with a bang."

Our eyes meet, and I know the moment she understands that I'm not talking about just tonight, because her features fall. Her brows crash together, and for a brief moment I think she might cry. But, because she's Ash and full of strength and surprises, she swallows down her apparent sadness and lifts her chin.

She takes a sudden step back, her robe sliding open to reveal her naked flesh to me. My cock is aching and straining to get to her. I tug at the knot of my tie, needing air to breathe. Seeing her so fucking tempting is calling to the beast inside me. I want to prowl over to her, pin her down, and take every last bit of her I can get. I want to savor these moments because soon they'll be gone.

"You'll know," she says finally. "You'll know when I've had enough, because you know me. I trust that when you know, you'll back off."

Her trust in me makes me feel like shit. Ash puts too much trust in the world. Too much trust in monsters like me. It's why they prey on her.

Then don't send her out into it, dumbass.

I hate that I will.

"Let's begin," I grit out as I shed my jacket. "On your knees, maid."

Her sassy eyebrow arches up in that bitchy way I love so much, but she wisely keeps her mouth shut. I yank off my tie as she allows her robe to slip off her shoulders, pooling at her feet. Then, she gracefully falls to her knees, her tits bouncing with the movement. Seeing her on her knees, naked and willing in my living room is nearly too much to bear. She's too perfect. A perfect sexual match for me. It's too bad everything else about her doesn't fit into my world.

I flick through my buttons, enjoying the way her hazel orbs darken with lust. She's just as obsessed with me as I am her. It's a lethal combination, because neither of us seems strong enough to keep the other one at bay. Each of us keeps falling into the same depraved trap.

Once I've shed my shirt, I prowl over to her. My erection, barely contained in my slacks, is in her pretty face.

"Dirty girls belong on the floor," I lightly smack her cheek. "Right?"

"Ten grand."

I smirk at her reply. "Expensive."

"You have the money."

Twisting my fingers in her hair, I yank her head back. "You're not worth it."

"Twenty grand. Easy money, Constantine."

My heart gallops in my chest. There's still so much I want to do to her—with her—but our time is done. After tonight, I need to regain my focus. Playtime is over.

"I think they call your kind gold diggers." I slide my hand to her throat, jerking her to her feet. "Am I right?"

A mixture of defiance and lust burn hot in her eyes. "Thirty."

"Take my pants off, whore." I squeeze on her neck, enjoying the way her face quickly turns purple.

"Forty," she rasps out and fumbles with my belt, undoing it blindly as her eyes are locked on mine.

I groan when her palm slides into my pants, rubbing against my throbbing cock. "Needy girl with daddy issues is all you are." I nip at her bottom lip hard enough she whines.

"Fifty." Her voice is a mere whisper because of the unrelenting grip I have on her neck.

As soon as I let go of her throat, she gets down to business of divesting me of my clothes. I allow her to remove my pants and boxers. Shoes and socks. When I'm naked, the tip of my cock leaking with pre-come, I grab a handful of her ass, yanking her to me.

"Eager slut, hmm?"

"Sixty."

A dark chuckle escapes me. "We might make a millionaire out of you by the end of the evening. Well played, Cinderelliott."

She preens at my praise.

This. Fucking. Girl.

To end her gloating, I throw her over my shoulder, smacking her ass hard enough she yelps. "Neediest brat I've ever met."

"Seventy!" she yells out, smacking my ass right back.

I fight a stupid smile as I stride into her room. Sex isn't supposed to be like this. It's not supposed to be… fun.

"Spread your legs and show me what I'm overpaying for," I order, tossing her on the bed.

"Eighty."

I smack her thigh. "Eighty now."

Her dark hair is wild around her, and her pouty pink lips are parted. I could spend hours devouring this woman. Every part of her is a piece I want to consume and live off until my dying days. I don't understand her or how she gets inside me like she does, but it's her superpower, that's for damn sure.

"Make love to me like this," she murmurs. "Where I can see your mean face the whole time."

A challenge.

She wants me to bite.

To be her hero and save the day.

I'm afraid the damn girl will never learn.

I grab her by the hips and flip her. "No."

She squeals when I smack her ass, chasing it with another insult. I pounce on her, nipping at her shoulder and neck, whispering more cruel words. Ash whines out each growing number to the total.

One hundred thousand.

Two.

Three.

Four.

Five.

Time passes too quickly. I'm inside her, already having tallied up half a million dollars. I fuck her rough and painfully, shoving her face against the mattress so I don't have to look at her. Because if I see her face, I'll back off. I'll rethink everything. I'll fucking pull her into my arms and hold onto something I shouldn't.

Her sobs only fuel me.

"Too much, Cinderelliott?"

"Never with you."

I wrap my hand around her throat, squeezing, as I remind her I'm the most powerful man in the city, and she's nothing but an employee. Worthless and insignificant.

It's all a fucking game, though.

My dick thinks she's the best damn thing it's ever encountered.

My heart aches for some goddamn reason.

My mind won't shut the fuck up, tossing out a million different ways she could fit into the complicated Constantine world.

The insults don't come, and my thrusting slows. I crave to flip her back over so I can stare into her intense hazel eyes. To worship her body for hours and hours. Spend a whole night fixated on her plump lips alone. Instead, I bite at her shoulder and call her a plaything to be used and discarded as I come into her tight, needy body.

Silence fills the air. All that can be heard is her bird singing in the living room and our heavy pants. My dick continues to throb though I've drained my release into her. I'm not sure if she climaxed or not. The pounding in my heart is so loud and painful it feels as though it's trying to beat its way out of my chest. The cacophony of thoughts storming around in my head is giving me a goddamn headache.

I've spent right at eight hundred grand for this filthy fuck.

Expensive, but worth it.

"How much?" she murmurs.

"Seven ninety."

"No." She tries to turn her head to look at me but can't. "How much for you to spend the night with me? I need—"

Sliding out of her body, I clamber off the bed, unable to look at her as she rolls onto her back. "A million."

"Win," she whines, sniffling as she reaches for me. "Take seven ninety."

"You may be the bargain around here," I bite out in a cruel tone, "but I'm still a fucking Constantine. No discounts for the poor."

Fresh tears form in her eyes, and her bottom lip wobbles. "You're an asshole."

I laugh, but it's hollow and hateful. "Tell me something we don't already know. Goodnight,

Ash. See yourself out. Use the 'whore' apartment until you find one on your own."

Her sobs echo behind me, chasing me like fucking ghosts. I stalk out of her room and up the stairs, eager to wash away the evidence of my evil. That's what I am. Evil fucking monster. Ash Elliott needs to run far, far away from the likes of me. What Mother can't accomplish in destroying her, I will. Whereas my mother will shred her life, I'll be the one to cut down Ash piece by piece and set her world ablaze until she's nothing but… ash.

The cold shower I find myself in seems like a fitting punishment. It strikes me relentlessly with icy pinpricks, reminding me that I deserve to feel the pain of it. Maybe my heart can't ever feel as it once did, but I still deserve to suffer as far as Ash is concerned. I still crave to ache for what I've done to her—what I will do to her. Right now, she's crying for a man who can never love her. Praying to god that I'll somehow change for her. Find a way to love and adore and keep her.

I can't.

But my stupid mind replays the heartbroken look on her face when I left her on the bed, naked and dripping with my come. All she wanted was a night in my arms. To feel safe and cared for. Loved.

Shutting off the shower, I snag a towel off the rack. Prissy warm towels my ass. I huff as I dry myself off, my mind unable to stop from going a hundred miles a second. I brush my teeth and comb out my hair, refusing to look at my reflection.

Sometimes I don't want to see the villain staring back at me.

Sometimes I wish, for once, I was the prince.

My eyes, on their own accord, lift to the mirror. Darkness and emptiness stare back at me. No princes here. Just a filthy, fucked-up king who broke the only good thing in his world.

I throw on some sweats, trying like hell to ignore the whimpering downstairs. My heart thunders inside my chest as I pace my bedroom. With a frustrated sigh, I stalk into my massive closet. All my suit jackets and slacks hang in perfect order aside from one. I walk over to it and straighten it, then I access my wall safe. After putting in the code, I bypass the stacks of money, heading right for the dumb coupon book. Flipping it open, I find the coupon I need and tear it out.

The man rushing downstairs like his life depends on it is not Winston Constantine. It's a weak boy who's worried about a girl—his girl. I shed the villain at the door to her bedroom that's now dark and slide beneath the covers. I shove the coupon into the palm of her hand, curling my own around hers, forcing her to crumple it into her fist. Her body is stiff as I inhale her hair and nuzzle her neck.

"Cuddle coupon," I murmur. "You said they never expire."

Her body relaxes, and a small, teary laugh escapes her. "Never."

"Next time, negotiate better, Ash," I say with a heavy sigh, squeezing her to me. "Please. I need you to." *Because I can't let you go. Not yet.*

She nods. "Next time?"

I was certain tonight would be the last time, but my dumbass is addicted to her. Just like I am to the stupid gummy bears. "Yeah, next time. I'm not done with you. You're not a millionaire yet. My investments always pay off."

"I'm more than an investment," she tells me, her voice shaking though she tries to be brave. "I'm just yours."

I don't argue with that.

Tomorrow, I can ream myself for being weak.

Right now, I'm her prince. Hers. Maybe only for a few hours, all of which we'll be sleeping. Regardless, it's what I'll be.

"Who's Layla?"

Her question is a cold rain of reality drenching me. "No one important." It's the truth, and I know she hears it in my tone. "No one like you."

"Good," she murmurs before her breathing becomes soft and rhythmic with sleep.

I don't fall asleep, though.

Because if I get to be a prince, even in the dark for just a few short hours, I want to be aware of it. I want to be present. I greedily take every second.

CHAPTER EIGHTEEN

ASH

I WAKE TO the smell of bacon, and my stomach grumbles. Francis scurries in with a tray of food, leaving it on the nightstand before rushing out. Winston is no longer in bed, though his masculine, soapy scent still lingers in the air. I sit up and pull the tray into my lap. It's then I notice my phone sitting beside me on the pillow he slept on.

After inhaling a few bites of eggs and bacon, I grab my phone to check for any missed messages.

> **Win:** *Emergency business meeting in Paris. Took Perry with me. It should be a quick meeting, but it needs to be done in person. I'll return Monday evening at the latest. I've emailed you with your education fund details as well. Don't let anyone in my house while I'm gone unless their last name is Constantine.*

Typical Winston. All business. No mention of the emotional night we had.

My heart aches at the memory. He'd been so cold when he came home. Distant and borderline cruel. But I thought like always, I could draw him out of his mind and into my arms to a place where we meet in the middle on even ground.

He wouldn't allow it.

His walls were high and made of steel. I know his mother played a part in it. Still, I couldn't help the way my heart physically hurt when he denied me his tenderness. Sure, I should have negotiated it up front, but I didn't. I'd thought—hoped—he'd soften for me. Instead, he left me sobbing.

But he came back.

Clean and offering a cuddle coupon.

Winston Constantine is a hard nut to crack, but I won't give up on him. His mother might think I'm beneath him or using him, but she's wrong. He and I match up in ways I can't explain. We just match. And with each passing day, I discover more and more about him that I want to know and protect.

He might be ready to give me up because I'm a threat to his cold heart, but I won't give him up without a fight.

Me: *Miss you already.*

His response is immediate. Five eyeroll emojis

in a row.

Win: *Needy.*

My heart squeezes in my chest. This feels right. Our playful banter. Teasing and taunting. Last night was a glitch. A hiccup. We'll continue on just like this.

Me: *Will you bring me back a souvenir?*

Win: *No.*

Me: *Pleassssse.*

Win: *Definitely no now.*

Me: *Don't make me beg your brother.*

Win: *Fine, Cinderelliott, I'll bring you back a postcard. Happy?*

Me: *I am now.*

I send him a bunch of heart-eyed emojis to drive him crazy. He doesn't respond so I finish breakfast and then hop in the shower. Once I'm clean and ready for the day, I check for any other messages. I see he's deposited the money I earned last night and sent me a selfie of him and Perry on what looks like a private jet. Perry is grinning and Winston is scowling, but they both still somehow look just alike.

I send him five hundred through Apple Pay for the selfie and then suggest I'll send him more if they want to get naked for the next pictures. Give him a taste of his own medicine. My text earns me several middle finger emojis that have me laughing. The next text that comes through, though, isn't Win.

> **Dad:** Dinner at five? I'm making your favorite.
>
> **Me:** Just the two of us?
>
> **Dad:** Family dinner. I know things have been difficult lately with you and your stepbrothers. I think that's me and Manda's fault. We should be nurturing a healthy relationship between our children. As it stands, I think the boys feel threatened by you. I just want to fix it so we can all be happy.

I curse as I reread his text. I do *not* want to have dinner with the stepmonsters and their wicked mother.

> **Me:** They assaulted me, Dad.

The dots move and stop several times before he finally replies.

> **Dad:** I know, honey, and I'm so sorry. I came down on them hard for it too. Threatened them within an inch of their lives. It caused a rift between me and Manda. Admittedly, I was ready to kill them. They know they're on thin ice.

A smile tugs at my lips as I imagine Dad bitching them out.

> **Me:** *Fine, but as soon as dinner is over, I'm going back to Winston's.*

Or my apartment. Because I have one of those now. A safe place to go if everything goes to hell. I'll never admit it to Winston, but I am sort of thankful to have it, even if I never go there. Just the fact that I could if I wanted to is enough.

> **Dad:** *I just miss you, but I know you're growing up. One day I'll blink and you'll be married with a family of your own. Probably with that Constantine since he's so adamant about spoiling you every chance he gets.*

Don't I wish. It's going to take a hell of a lot of convincing to get Winston even on the same page as being my boyfriend. I can see through his teasing. I'm not *really* his—not how I want to be.

> **Me:** *He's my employer. Don't start planning a wedding yet.*
>
> **Dad:** *He's more than that and we all know it. Be careful with him, honey. A man like him could destroy the heart of a girl like you.*

Too late.

My heart is in Winston's hands, and he'll be

the ultimate decider on what happens to it.

Me: *See you at five.*

✧   ✧   ✧

I WALK INTO the brownstone, my armor on and bitchy attitude in place. The triplets will want me cowering, but I refuse to let them see me afraid. Dad and Manda will be here so it's not like they'll do anything. If this had happened to Winston, he sure as hell wouldn't hide from them. He'd face them head on and look them in the eyes.

I'll get them back eventually.

"In here, sweetheart," Dad calls from the kitchen.

I follow my nose to where he's standing at the stove, stirring his homemade Alfredo sauce. It reminds me of when I was a girl and Mom would be standing beside him, teasing him about the only meal he could cook. I'd giggle and tell her that he could make frozen waffles too, which, looking back, didn't really help his case.

God, I miss her.

I hug Dad from behind, resting my cheek on his solid back. He's not a beast of power like Winston, but he's steady and solid, powerful in his own right. There's something to be said about the strength of a father. Knowing he chewed out the triplets has me relaxing.

"Smells good. But can it possibly be as good as your frozen waffles?" I tease, smiling when he chuckles.

"There's no comparison to my frozen waffles. Why don't you grab the stuff to make a salad?"

I release him to busy myself pulling out the ingredients. For a moment, I can almost pretend it's just the two of us back in our old apartment. Sometime after Mom and before Manda. When we were each other's entire world. He whistles a familiar tune while I cut tomatoes for the salad.

"Smells delicious," Manda says, entering the kitchen and cooling it several degrees. "Hello, Ash."

I give her a wave with the knife in my hand, not meeting her hard stare. The sloppy sounds of their kissing kill any happy moments I'd enjoyed a few seconds before.

"Will the boys be joining us?" Dad asks, his voice low and tight with tension.

"Yes. Just as we discussed. This dinner is important." She sighs and then pats me on the back. "Everything will work out just fine, right, sweetie?"

I cringe at the endearment but manage to nod my head. Dad seems hellbent on making things right in this family, so I won't argue. I doubt either Dad or Manda can convince the Terror Triplets to stop being psychos, but I suppose it's worth a try.

"Hey, sis," a deep voice booms.

Swiveling around, I glare at the new arrival. Sully. The nicest of the three, but not by much. His dark brow lifts at the sight of the knife in my hand.

"Don't stab me." He grins, playful and charming, as though he and his brothers didn't cut my dress from my body and rob me blind.

Manda frowns in disapproval at me. Dad puffs out his chest and squeezes Sully's shoulder hard enough to make him wince.

"Want me to hold him so you can get your revenge?" Dad asks, his smile a little on the evil side.

Manda gasps, and I crack up laughing at the sight of Sully's wide eyes. I pretend to think about it for a second and then shake my head.

"Maybe later. After dessert," I say before turning back to the salad.

Manda and Sully chat about what new cars they're going to get next since theirs were destroyed last weekend. I personally think they should have to Uber everywhere, but no one asks for my opinion. Sparrow joins us, and like Sully, pretends he's a stellar stepbrother. They both take turns ribbing Dad about his favorite football team, the Patriots, and how they'll never make it to the Super Bowl. I help Dad by setting the table, and Manda assists him by bringing the food over. She then pours wine for all of us. Scout's empty seat has me relaxing even more.

Through dinner, Sully and Sparrow turn on the charm. A few times, they almost have me convinced that they're done being assholes. Almost. I'll never fully let down my guard with those three, especially Scout. Luckily, according to the guys, he was meeting up with a friend so he couldn't be at dinner. It's almost pleasant when I tune out Manda and her boys, enjoying my time with Dad. I'm just helping Dad clean up the kitchen when Manda gets a call.

"What?" She holds a hand to her chest, blinking hard in shock. "Did they take anything?" A pause. "Oh no." Another pause. "We'll be right there."

"What is it?" Dad demands.

"The Baldridge building," Manda says with a frown. "Several offices were broken into, including mine. Files have been rifled through. I need to get up there and talk to the police."

My heart stutters at the mention of the Baldridge building. Of all the times I've heard Manda speak about her office, not once do I remember her ever stating the name of the building. It makes me wonder if Winston knows she has her office there. It certainly makes sense as to how she would know Meredith, though, since it's her husband's name on the building.

"Go," I mutter to Dad. "She needs you. I'll finish up cleaning and then head out myself."

Dad glowers at Sully and Sparrow. "I can trust you two to behave?"

Both of them nod before hugging Manda.

"Need help cleaning?" Sully asks.

I shrug and then hug Dad. "Text me later and let me know how it went."

He kisses my forehead, and then they're gone. Sully and Sparrow don't pounce on me like I expect. I'm thankful I decided to leave my phone and purse at Winston's. There was no way in hell I was taking another chance with them stealing my things again. I brought enough cash with me in case of an emergency, but it's stowed safely in the glovebox of the Escalade along with my driver's license. My keys are also inside the truck, because I can access the vehicle through a touchpad on the door. I was prepared this time.

With the Terror Triplets, you always have to be one step ahead.

Sparrow leaves the kitchen, and Sully continues to help me clean up. We don't speak or look at each other. I'm just wiping off the stove when the front door closes. My head snaps over to look at Sully who's smirking.

And that's my cue to leave.

I drop the dishrag onto the counter and walk out of the kitchen without so much as a goodbye. Luckily, I don't encounter anyone along the way. I open the front door but a strong hand slaps on it, slamming it shut.

Whirling around with my heart in my throat, I meet the pissed-off glare of Scout.

Fuck.

Lifting my chin, I meet his dark stare. "Leave me alone."

"No can do, sis," he growls. "I went to too much trouble to get you right here by yourself."

I narrow my eyes. "You stole from your own mother?"

His chuckle is low and without humor. "I messed her office up a bit, but I didn't steal anything. I'm not a monster." He lifts his hand to toy with a strand of my hair.

I smack it away. "Don't touch me."

"Aww," Scout mocks, "it's cute how you think you have a say."

Before I can try and escape, he pounces on me. All too easily, Scout uses his strength against me, overpowering me before I take my next breath. I let out a shriek from beneath his palm as he carries me up the stairs. My heart is racing inside my chest as I wonder how in the hell I'll get out of here.

I kick out, trying to find purchase on anything, but end up swiping empty air. Scout bypasses my room and takes me straight for his. A terrified mewl crawls up my throat to find Sully and Sparrow inside waiting.

Scout tosses me on the bed, and I scramble to my knees, eyeing the door behind him.

"Dad will be back soon," I warn, my voice shaking with fear. "He'll kill you if you touch me."

"He's not going to find out," Scout barks back, "because I'll send your dirty sex videos to everyone on his client list." His smile is sinister. "He leaves his computer unlocked all the time. All it took was once to download what I needed to a flash drive."

"So?" I hiss. "You think I'll bend over and take it because you threaten me?"

Sparrow snorts. "You have no choice."

"Fuck you," I spit out. "You promised Dad you wouldn't hurt me."

"Sully and I both did," he agrees. "But no one said anything about Scout."

I launch myself off the bed in an attempt to make it to the door, but Scout is faster. He body slams me onto the bed before he starts pawing at me. I know he's looking for my phone, but he won't find it. As soon as he realizes I don't have anything on me, his features harden. Like a switch goes off, he starts yanking at my T-shirt.

"If you touch me, I'll tell them you forced me," I choke out. "You'll go to prison."

Scout sneers at me. "And who will they believe? Three boys just being boys, having sex with a girl they find attractive? Or a prostitute who fucks rich old dudes for money?"

"You said we were just going to—" Sully starts, but Scout cuts him off by barking out his name.

"Help me get her clothes off," Scout orders.

I scream and squirm as the three of them work together. I manage to kick Sparrow in the nose and Sully in the balls, but in the end, they strip me and hold me down. The sobs escaping me sound more like desperate gasps of air. Like a fish on the banks of a river writhing under the paw of a tiger.

Scout produces a Sharpie and begins to write on my stomach. Where it once said Winston's Dirty Whore, it now says Scout's Slutty Sister. They laugh as they take turns writing crude things on me. But, aside from the words, they haven't violated me in ways that might send them to prison.

"Text her boyfriend," Scout orders Sully. "Tell him what we want. In return, we'll let her go."

I glower at Scout as Sully snaps pictures of me. Then, his fingers fly over the keys as he no doubt sends his demands to Winston. Several long minutes go by with no response.

"He's in a meeting, dumbass," I hiss at Scout, tears leaking down my temples.

Time drags on as we wait.

"Text him and tell him he has five minutes to respond or else I'm going to fuck his pretty whore." Scout smiles at me like the damn devil, stopping my heart in the process. "And then we'll send him a video."

"Please don't do this," I beg.

Five long minutes pass by with the boys laughing and me tearfully begging. Finally, Sully says, "He responded."

"What did he say?" Scout demands.

Sully frowns. "He doesn't negotiate with terrorists."

"Fucking asshole," Scout roars, launching himself at me.

I let loose a blood-curdling scream as Scout starts to undo his jeans. I catch Sully's wide-eyed stare and beg for him to save me. Sparrow curses and paces beside the bed.

"Dude, we said scare her, not this," Sully says to Scout.

"Shut the fuck up," Scout bites back. "Constantine wants to play fucking chicken, then we'll play fucking chicken." As soon as his dick is in his hand, I close my eyes. I can't do this. I can't be mentally present for this.

But, instead of him violating me, I hear sweet music to my ears.

Police sirens.

Scout scrambles to dress, and I realize I'm safe. Winston called the police. All the way from halfway across the world, he saved me.

The pounding on the front door has me sucking in a breath of relief.

Thank god.

CHAPTER NINETEEN

WINSTON

PISSED OFF DOESN'T even begin to describe how I feel right now.

Infuriated. Maddened. Rage-filled. Near a nuclear meltdown.

I'm about to explode with the need to murder those fucking animals. Especially Scout. I should be doing damage control on the massive account we just lost, but instead, I can't stop thinking about her.

Is she safe?

Did they hurt her?

Why the fuck was she over there?

"Keaton just texted me," Perry says from beside me on the plane. "He and Tinsley are at your place now with Ash."

It's been a full fourteen hours since I got the text with a picture of my girl once again in the clutches of those motherfuckers along with a demand to get them back into Harvard. Rather than playing their games since I was all the way in goddamn France, I immediately called the police. I couldn't risk it. I'll get those assholes back in a way that hurts, but at that moment, all I could think about was making sure she was safe.

I left the meeting that had gone late into the night where millions were at stake to turn around and fly back to New York. I'd expected Perry to tell me what a bad fucking idea it was because it's one of our big accounts, and one he'd been working on, but he'd been just as eager as I was to get back to the city.

On the flight back, I didn't sleep a wink. All I could do was stare at the picture they texted me. Reread the threat over and over again.

It's not enough that they were arrested.

Their rich mommy bailed them out as soon as she could.

This incident is but a blip for them.

For me, it's more than a blip. It's a bomb that exploded on me and everything I thought I knew. I'd struggled with whatever it is me and Ash are, but in that moment, seeing her in their grasp, I lost my fucking head.

She's mine.

Not theirs or her father's or anyone's.

Mine.

Everything my mother tried to drill into my head at dinner a couple of nights ago has long been forgotten. I'm clearly an idiot when it comes to Ash Elliott, and I can't find it in me to care.

The stewardess lets us know we can depart the plane in just a few more minutes. Our car is waiting. Within the hour I'll be home with Ash back in my arms. I'm wound up so tight I feel like I could snap at any second. I know I won't calm my ass down until I see with my own two eyes she's safe.

"Manda should have let them rot in jail," Perry grumbles from beside me. "From what Keaton says, her dad is pissed."

"Pissed?" I spit out, turning to glare at my brother. "I'm *pissed* he left her alone with those fucking monsters."

"That's basically what he told her dad. That if he couldn't keep her safe, we Constantines could."

"We?"

Perry shrugs. "We like Ash too. You think Keaton was going to let her stay there where those assholes live?"

It pleases me to have my siblings on my side. We may not always see eye to eye but when someone fucks with our own, we stand in solidarity. And since Ash is mine, my brothers and youngest sister have my back.

I make a call to Ulrich, our private investigator, while we wait to deboard the plane.

"Ulrich speaking," he rasps out, his voice abused from a lifetime of chain smoking.

"I want everything you can dig up on Manda Mannford. Everything."

His chuckle turns into a smoker's cough. "Wanna know what brand of toilet paper she wipes her ass with too?"

"Everything," I reiterate. "I don't want anything left out."

"On it, Boss."

I may have shown weakness by calling the cops on those snakes, but it was a temporary solution to my problem. I'm only getting started on my retaliation. They're going to feel violated like she felt violated when I fuck their lives so hard they have no choice but to become my compliant bitches.

The alternative for them is the fucking grave.

✧   ✧   ✧

I WALK INTO my condo, dropping my bag just inside the door, and storm into the living room. Ash sits beside Tinsley, curled up in a blanket, her bird cradled in her hands. As soon as she locks eyes with me, the fierce façade she'd somehow formed crumbles away revealing the sad, broken girl. I drop down on the other side of her, grab her hips, and haul her into my lap.

"I'm here, baby," I rumble, kissing the top of her head. "You're safe now."

Baby?

I ignore that endearment, but I know Ash heard it because she starts to cry, clinging to my chest. Shrimp chirps loudly and skitters up the front of my jacket to my shoulder as if to tattle on the triplets right in my fucking ear.

I know, bird. I fucking know.

Keaton's brows are at his hairline as he watches me hold Ash. He has to know by now that Ash is more than some employee. She's so much more. Just because I'm in denial or can't articulate it doesn't change that fact. My smart brother certainly doesn't miss a thing.

"Mother isn't to know about this," I say to Perry as he plops down beside Keaton.

"That you're in love?" he taunts, grinning at me.

Ash lets out a teary laugh and then smiles at me. "What's that? You're in looooove?"

I roll my eyes at the way she draws out the

word, which sets Tinsley off into a fit of giggles. Despite these assholes teasing me, I'm happy Ash isn't completely ruined by the Mannford triplets.

"Lust, Cinderelliott. I'm in lust. Happy?"

She cackles and kisses my lips. "Very."

Shrimp sings and flaps his wings. Then he sets to pecking at my head behind my ear. Damn bird likes to look for bugs in my hair. Ash says it's his way of taking care of me. I think it's fucking weird.

"Never thought I'd see the day where Winston lets a bird peck at his head," Perry says with great amusement. "This is hilarious."

I flip him off and then pull the bird off my shoulder. After stroking his little head, I tell him to leave me alone. Shrimp sings and then flaps all the way up to my chandelier, otherwise known as his damn playground.

"I'm being serious," I say again to Perry. "Mother meddles too much. I can handle my own shit."

"What exactly are you handling?" Ash asks, frowning at me.

"Those bastards."

"How?" Her hazel eyes flash with fury. Not at me. At them. She wants to make them pay. Well, that makes two of us.

"In ways that'll hurt. In ways their mommy can't buy their way out of."

"Do I want to know?" she asks.

"It's probably best if you don't. Plausible deniability."

Plus, Ash doesn't have a poker face. I don't need her getting her own ass in trouble because she wears her thoughts for all to see.

"Where does your father stand in all of this?" I run my finger down the length of her arm, enjoying the way she shivers, completely forgetting we have a baby Constantine audience until Keaton sniggers.

"Dad is livid," she says with a sigh. "He said that if Manda chooses the triplets side on this, he'll be forced to choose mine." She leans her head on my shoulder. "I hate that he's even put in this position."

I don't remind her that he got himself there in the first place by pursuing the damn woman.

"Hmm," is all I say.

"That's the hmm that means people will suffer," Perry reveals a little too gleefully.

"Fuck off."

"Usually it's me he's punishing," Ash tattles. "It's about time he let me on Team Constantine."

"You're not on the team," I mutter.

"Kinda," she argues to which Tinsley laughs.

"You're like the bat boy. But with tits."

She smacks me. "More like the mascot."

"Since when did the Constantine mascot turn into a poor maid who fishes for compliments?"

"Since now." Ash smirks at me. "Or I could be the cheerleader."

A wolfish grin splits my face. "I'm okay with that."

"I'm sure I have some cheerleader uniforms in the back seat of my car," Perry offers, waggling his brows like he's the shit.

Keaton snorts out a laugh. "That makes you sound like a pervert."

"I *am* a pervert."

Me and Ash both laugh. The only real perverts in this room are the two of us. The little Constantines are just wannabe perverts.

"Okay, assholes," I grunt, rising to my feet with Ash still in my arms. "Go home to your mommy. I have much-needed sleep to catch up on."

"She's your mommy too, dumbass," Perry throws back.

I ignore him and carry Ash into her room, kicking the door shut behind us. She sticks her tongue out at me when I unceremoniously drop her onto the bed. While she scoots under the covers, I shed out of my suit down to my boxers, following her into the bed.

"Where's my damn coupon?" I ask, hauling her to my chest so I can inhale her hair.

"The cuddle coupon that you already used?"

"That's the one."

"You can't use it again. That's not how coupons work."

I kiss her neck. "Then how much does this thing we're doing cost?"

She lets out a sigh. "It's free. Consider it a handout for the needy boy."

"Brat."

"You like it when I'm bratty."

Indeed, I do.

The apartment grows quiet, which means my siblings left. Even Shrimp is being quiet. My eyes drift closed as sleep overtakes me. I'm tired as fuck and jetlagged. It's late morning but it may as well be two a.m. for how exhausted I am.

"Win?"

"Hmm?"

"Thank you."

"For what?"

"For being you."

"You're sappy when you're sad," I remark, my

voice thick with sleep.

"I'm not sad anymore." A beat of silence and then she speaks again. "Goodnight, Constantine."

"It's morning, Cinderelliott."

"Still good."

"Hmph. That's a stretch."

"It's good now," she amends.

I can't argue with that.

CHAPTER TWENTY

ASH

I SET MY phone down, still smiling from Winston's last text, so I can pull my hair into a ponytail. We've been teasing back and forth in between his meetings this morning. Apparently, something big went down with one of his clients in Paris, and he's been doing damage control ever since. Where I was exhausted this morning after the hellacious weekend I had, Win was fresh-faced and ready to work come Monday morning. I'd tried to find the motivation to go to work, but he shut it down and told me to take the day off.

My phone continues to buzz with texts. Once my hair is fixed, I pick it back up to see what else the dirty boy has to say.

I deflate at seeing Dad's text.

Dad: Come home, honey. Manda and the boys aren't here. It's safe now.

It's been one variation or another of this since

the triplets were arrested on Saturday night. I understand Dad is worried about me, but I don't feel as though he did his best to protect me from them. He let his guard down, and they swooped in.

Me: *I have my own apartment now. I'm safe there.*

Even if I never use it, at least I have it. Plus, Dad needs to know I'm not going back there, and I certainly don't need him to protect me. I'll protect myself.

My phone rings, but I don't recognize the number. I ignore it and head into the living room to check on Shrimp. Tucked into the bars of his cage is a postcard with a picture of the Eiffel Tower on it. On the back, in Winston's fancy flourishes, it says:

Dinner tonight, girlfriend. – W

Not a question. Just a typical Winston demand. But also sweet and romantic… for him. I laugh, holding it to my chest and then sigh happily. I'm not sure what will become of us, but I don't see it ending anytime soon. This weekend only seemed to solidify our bond.

My phone rings again. I answer it in case it's

Winston. Not many people have this new number.

"Hello?"

"Miss Elliott?" a female says in a curt tone.

"Yes?"

"This is Caroline Constantine." She pauses to let that name sink in, and boy does it sink, bottoming out my stomach. "Meet me at Carmichael's Day Spa in an hour."

I'm stunned silent as I wonder how in the hell she got my number. Furthermore, how does she know I'm not at work and able to even go to the spa? I'm pretty confident Winston didn't seek out his mother to tell her all this. In fact, he seemed pretty adamant about keeping things from her.

"I, uh," I start but she cuts me off with a sharp sigh that reminds me of her eldest son.

"I'll send a car for you."

Beep-beep-beep.

She hung up on me. Lovely. At least I know where Winston got his winning personality from. I suck in a deep calming breath to steady myself. If I can handle Win, I can handle his mother. I refuse to let her intimidate me. Quickly, I shoot him a text.

> **Me:** *I've been summoned to a spa day with your mother. Should I be scared?*

Win: *Very.*

Me: *Ha. Seriously. I'm freaking out.*

Win: *I'm sure you'll figure it out.*

Me: *Gee, thanks. Send me to the wolves with no way to defend myself!*

Win: *Just one wolf.*

Me: *What if she tells me to stay away from you?*

Win: *Since when do you listen to anyone?*

Me: *I want to make a good impression.*

Win: *You're so old fashioned, Cinderelliott. Cute.*

Me: *You're patronizing me.*

Win: *Tell her you're my girlfriend. I'm sure that will go over wonderfully.*

Me: *I hate you.*

Win: *That's not a very nice thing to say to your boyfriend.*

Me: *Not my boyfriend.*

Win: *Good. Now you're prepared for Mother.*

I send him a million eyeroll emojis. He replies back with a breadstick emoji. Asshole.

✦　　✦　　✦

CARMICHAEL'S DAY SPA is one of the fanciest places I've ever been to. Rather than your typical spa—earthy, organic vibes—this one screams money with its high-end chandeliers and ornate furniture. Wearing a pair of cutoff shorts, my flip flops, and a Columbia University T-shirt Dad got me when I was accepted, I feel incredibly out of place. I gnaw on my fingernail as I wait for Caroline to arrive. I'm hoping she'll stand me up and I can go back to Winston's.

The door opens to the spa and my hopes are dashed.

In walks Caroline Constantine in a smart pastel ensemble with an air of authority swirling in along with her expensive floral scent. She pushes her oversized sunglasses up over her head, revealing her sharp, penetrating blue eyes.

"Miss Elliott," she greets, a fake smile plastered on her face. "Thank you for meeting me."

Like I had a choice, lady.

I stand and awkwardly shuffle toward her. "No problem."

Her gaze roams over my outfit, and her nostrils flare. "Darlene," she calls out. "We're ready."

Darlene, a woman with a severe bun and perfect makeup, scampers over to us. "Come this way, ladies. We have your room ready."

I follow after the women, trying and failing to calm my nerves. I'm not sure why in the hell this woman wants to have a spa day with me, but something tells me I'll soon find out. Her cold demeanor doesn't give me much confidence that it'll be a fun girls' day. Darlene escorts us into a room with two overstuffed armchairs and armoires beside each.

"You'll find your robes and slippers in here," Darlene says, gesturing to one of the armoires. "Cindy will be by with some refreshments after you've gotten comfortable. Padre and Evan are preparing the massage room for you."

She leaves me alone with Caroline. The woman turns her back to me and begins undressing. Since I don't care a thing about seeing this woman naked, I quickly undress and pull on the robe. Once the slippers are on and my things are stowed away, I sit down in one of the comfy chairs. As soon as she sits, a woman who must be Cindy, slips into the room with a tray. She hands us each a flute of champagne and sits a cheese and fruit board down between us on a small table. Then, she's gone, once again leaving me in awkward silence with Win's mother.

"This place is lovely," I mutter, unsure what to even talk about.

"Indeed." She smirks at me and sips her champagne.

She reminds me so much of Win in this moment, I bite back a smile.

"Something funny?" Her blue eyes are hard and probing. Yep, definitely just like Win.

"You just remind me of him is all." My smile breaks free. "Your mannerisms are a lot alike."

Her features soften almost imperceptibly. But, since I'm good at reading Winston, I notice the tiny change in her. Point one for me. She apparently loves talking about her children. Okay, so "loves" might be a stretch. I'm not sure the Constantines love anything but their last name.

"What are you doing with my son?" All warmth has evaporated as her chilly words send a shiver down my spine.

"He's my boyfriend," I blurt out and then cringe.

This time, she's better about schooling her emotions. She doesn't flinch or move. "Boyfriend?" A heavy sigh escapes her. "Oh, you silly girl."

My skin heats at her patronizing tone.

"Here I thought you were out for your own personal agenda, but I can see it's not that at all, is it?" She doesn't wait for me to respond. "You really do like my son. You really do believe he's your boyfriend."

I straighten my spine, pinning her with a hard stare. "I don't have an agenda—"

"Besides having Winston pay for your education?" Her sculpted brow arches up.

Shame burns through me, but I refuse to cower. "That was Winston's idea, not mine." Seriously, how does this lady know everything?

"Winston seems to have a lot of 'ideas' where you're concerned."

"What can I say, I'm inspiring," I deadpan, my irritation bleeding through in my tone.

"Hmm."

Geez, here we go with the hmms.

"He does that too, you know," I mutter. "Perry says that when you decode the hmms, they actually mean you're about to make someone suffer."

Her eyes brighten at the mention of Perry, amusement briefly flashing in her expression. "Did he now?"

"I think he's onto something. Even Keaton does the hmm when he's mad." I grin despite being in the dragon's lair with her fire breathing down my neck. "Though, I haven't heard Tinsley do it. She seems like she's the nicest."

"Nicer than Perry?"

Gotcha, lady. You love your kids. I found your

Achilles heel.

"It's a tossup," I agree. "Perry did rescue me the night of Win's party."

"You were there?" She knows. Despite asking, she knows. I can see it in her intelligent gaze.

"Tinsley let me borrow a dress." I shrug. "And a wig."

"I see." She sips her champagne as though deep in thought. "What's a poor maid doing fraternizing with my children?"

Winston is his mother made over. Jesus.

"I told them I'm Team Constantine. Win said I could be the bat boy. Perry thinks he has a cheerleader outfit I can borrow. But I think I'm the mascot."

She blinks hard as she studies me. "You've all discussed this? In great detail?"

"They're great people," I tell her, meeting her stare. "Win, Perry, Keaton, Tinsley. Twice now your youngest children have come to my aid. And Winston?" I can't help but smile like a goofy lovestruck teenager. "He's a regular Prince Charming. Except when he's being a total asshole."

She smirks but hides it with the palm of her hand. "Excuse me?"

"We both know he can be," I throw back,

daring her to argue. "But it's one of his endearing qualities."

Our conversation is cut short when Darlene fetches us to lead us to the massage room. Caroline and I don't continue with an audience. I do my best to relax, but it's hard when your new boyfriend's mother who already hates you is half naked beside you. After massages, we go to individual sauna rooms and once we've sweat out all our toxins, we're led to private showers. Once I'm clean and feeling like jelly, Darlene reappears to show me to a salon area where Caroline is already sitting.

"Winston tells me he's taking you to dinner tonight," Caroline says, her eyes never leaving her reflection in the mirror.

"He is," I admit. "Did you speak to him?"

"Just now." She cuts her eyes my way. "After you've been made up, he's asked me to drop you at a dress shop not far from here."

I want to kill him. It's one thing for us to play our kinky little games together, but now his mother knows I let him dress me sometimes. My skin burns with embarrassment, but I smile at her in acknowledgment.

We spend the next couple of hours getting our hair trimmed, blown out, and styled. Then, the stylists apply makeup on us. It's strange to have a spa day with this woman, but it hasn't been horrible if I'm honest with myself.

"It's a pity Maggie died," Caroline says once we exit the building. "She was so young."

I stop dead in my tracks, snapping my head to her. "You knew my mother?"

Her expression is unreadable as she steps closer. "I know everything, Miss Elliott."

"But did you *know* her?" My voice wobbles and tears threaten. "Was she your friend?"

"Not her, no," she admits, her blue eyes sharp as they assess me. "I knew Barb personally, though."

I frown at her. "Who's Barb?"

We continue to stare at one another—her searching my gaze for something, and me just trying to figure out what she's talking about.

"Hmm," she mutters, picking a piece of lint off my shirt. "You weren't close to your grandmother?"

Oh… that Barb. Barbara Huffington. My mom's mother.

"Never met her. She passed away when I was little."

"I see." She pauses as though she wants to say more but bites her tongue in the end. "Well, it's a small world, isn't it? Let's get you dropped off."

"We forgot to pay," I remind her, gesturing back to the spa.

"Don't be silly." She ushers me into the car. I settle on the seat and try not to fidget as she scrutinizes me. The driver takes off without warning, making my stomach dip. As soon as I recognize the area we're in, I tap on the glass partition.

"Yes, miss?" the driver asks.

"Can we stop at the candy shop on the next block?"

"Of course."

I turn back around to discover Caroline's lips pressed together in a grim line. Ignoring her evident annoyance, I hop out of the car as soon as it stops, promising to be right back. Once inside, I get more red gummy bears for Winston since he's grown so fond of them. I grab a few more things and am checking out when my phone rings.

"Hello?"

"Ash Elliott. Lovely hearing your voice again."

The blood drains out of my face. "Leo."

"Did you miss me?"

The cashier gives me my change back, and I rush away from her to one corner of the store, my bags looped on my arm.

"What do you want?" I hiss into the phone.

"Same thing as last time. More information."

"Which I don't have."

"You spent the day with Caroline Constantine. Don't fucking lie to me."

My skin crawls at the thought of him watching me right now. Knowing exactly what I'm doing and who I'm with. Fucking stalker.

"We're not exactly chummy," I snap. "This is ridiculous, you know. I don't have what you want, and I can't get it."

He chuckles. "You'll get it or else everyone in this damn town will learn how tarnished the great Winston Constantine is. A dirty bastard in the bedroom who gets off on defiling little girls."

"I'm not a little girl."

"What happened in Paris?"

Jesus. This fucking guy.

"I don't know," I growl, losing patience. "I don't know anything!"

"Find out. I need to know what Winston is up to."

"Or else?"

"I'll ruin him and the entire family. I'll take down yours while I'm at it. Remember, click and click. That's all it'll take before the entire world will see the great Winston Constantine tearing your pretty asshole to shreds."

Bile rises in my throat at the image of that video on every television across the globe.

"Your threats are getting old." My false bravado is apparent when my voice quavers.

"They're promises, sweetheart, and I always make good on those. Get me more information."

He hangs up on me.

Bastard.

I'm rattled and stressed out by the time I make it back to the car. As soon as I'm seated, I fish out a bag of red gummy bears and hand them to Caroline.

"What's this?" Her lip curls up as though she's insulted.

"Win loves them. He's all out so I grabbed him some more. I took a chance that you might like them as well." I shrug and smile. "It's a thank you for today."

She blinks hard several times before tucking the bag away in her purse. "Hmm."

I can't help but giggle because, again, she reminds me of Winston when she does that.

Her blue eyes soften, and amusement briefly dances in them before she looks out the window, her wicked witch mask back in place. "You may be able to tempt my son with sweets, but you must realize he'll never marry you, never have you as anything more than a toy he plays with when he gets bored."

I swallow hard. That escalated quickly.

"I love my son, but I'm telling you this not only for his sake, but for yours." She pins me with a narrow stare. "Any designs you have on him, drop them. Do it now before you get even deeper. You're already in over your head." With that, she turns toward the window, her face in beautiful profile as I try to keep my emotions in check. All the lightness I thought I'd created is gone, and I realize Caroline has many layers—some warm, many cold, and all a mystery.

We ride in silence, and I text Winston to let him know I survived. I also need to feel his strength after dealing with Leo.

> **Me:** I'm alive to tell the tale…
>
> **Win:** Surprising.
>
> **Me:** You better take me someplace good for dinner since I just took one for the team.
>
> **Win:** The team, huh?
>
> **Me:** Team Constantine.
>
> **Win:** I was thinking Italian for dinner. Fancy a breadstick, Cinderelliott?
>
> **Me:** You're an asshole.

Win: *It's like you're surprised.*

This time, in a role reversal, he sends me heart eye emojis to which I respond with middle finger ones.

Winston Constantine is an asshole, but he's the asshole I'm falling helplessly for.

CHAPTER TWENTY-ONE

WINSTON

WHAT IS MY mother doing? She's not nice for no reason. She doesn't take people out for spa days. She's up to something. Eventually, I'll find out what it is. I'm just thankful Ash seemed to have made it out unscathed.

My phone buzzes from an incoming text.

Xavier: *We have what you asked for.*

Triumph surges through my veins, and I nearly knock my desk chair over in my haste to stand up. I grab my bag and lock my office.

"Leaving early, Mr. Constantine?" Deborah asks, a curious expression on her face.

"I have business to take care of."

I walk straight over to Perry's office, but it's empty. I find him sitting in Nate's office, peering at a notebook that's resting on his knee while Nate taps away on the computer.

"Perry, time to go," I bark out.

He nearly knocks his notebook onto the floor and rushes to his feet. Nate frowns, his gaze darting between us.

"Important meeting?" Nate asks.

"Something like that." I smirk. "Hold down the fort."

Nate frowns, but I don't stick around to explain. Perry grabs his bag, locks his office door, and then we're headed to the parking garage.

"I'll drive," he offers, laughing when I grimace. "What? I drive great."

"It's not how you drive. It's what you drive."

He whistles, unaffected by my insults as we climb into his orange abomination. The engine is loud, echoing off the parking garage walls, sounding like there are twenty muscle cars in a row, not just his. As he backs out of his parking spot and then peels out, gaining speed quickly, a thrill shoots down my spine. This car might be ugly as fuck, but it rides like a beast. He turns on some classic seventies rock as we drive to our destination. I nearly roll my eyes at how fucking corny he can be sometimes. "Cherry Bomb" by The Runaways blares through the speakers, and this idiot sings along, banging on the steering wheel like he's a drummer in the damn band.

I try my damnedest to ignore my brother, my mind scattered in a hundred different directions.

"Barracuda" by Heart comes on next, and Perry grins at me. His excitement is infectious. I smirk back at him. We discussed this moment in great detail on the plane ride back from Paris. I wasn't sure how long we'd have to wait, but my men are pretty good at doing what they're told, especially when you throw a huge bonus in if they can deliver sooner rather than later.

Perry guns it down the road, weaving in and out of traffic, making my heart thunder in my chest. He wrecks boats for fuck's sake. I don't trust his driving, especially in a car like a '69 Chevelle with more power under the hood than a boat could dream of. Thankfully, rather than killing us, he turns his blinker on like a good boy and darts his vehicle into a parking garage of a building we own.

He sings along loudly when "Just What I Needed" by The Cars comes on. I have to hold on to the dash to keep from flying all over the place as he drives around and around, taking us higher up the parking garage to the top level. Since the building is being renovated, there aren't any cars. But when we reach the top level, a black Mercedes SUV waits parked next to a white Porsche

Cayenne.

He kills the engine, thankfully ending his obnoxious singing. We climb out and walk over to the SUV where Xavier and Todd are waiting. Both men are dressed in black T-shirts, black jeans, and black boots. They're ex-Navy Seals and mean-ass motherfuckers. And on my payroll. Naturally. Only the best for the Constantines.

"You have what I asked for?" I raise a brow at Xavier.

"It's insulting you even have to ask." Xavier laughs and motions to the other side of the SUV.

Perry and I walk around to discover that Xavier and Todd delivered. Times three, in fact. Seeing the three little fuckfaces in the flesh, after what they did and tried to do to Ash, has anger exploding inside of me. I want to beat the fuck out of each of them.

But that's how a Morelli would do shit.

I'm a Constantine. We're classy.

"Aww, look what we have here," I taunt, squatting down in front of one of the triplets who's hogtied and glaring at me. "The ringleader. Scout."

Where the other two boys are terrified, Scout is pissed. If looks could kill, there's no doubt in my mind this psychopath would end me.

"You know why you're here?" I poke his forehead, enjoying his snarl. "Oh, that's right. You can't talk with tape over your mouth."

Perry laughs from behind me.

"Looks like you'll just have to listen, then," I say to the fuckwit. "You should have stayed the fuck away when I told you to."

His eyes burn into me, but they're growing glassy by the minute. Based on how the other two boys aren't struggling anymore, I estimate that I'm running out of time to get my point across.

"It's like this," I explain, shaking my head as though Scout is a naughty child who needs scolding. "You fucked up. Royally. Then, you thought you could best me. A fucking Constantine. Like a little bitch, you waited until I was away before you pounced on *my girlfriend*." I inwardly roll my eyes at the thought of Ash preening at my girlfriend comment. "You hurt her. You hurt what's mine."

Scout's eyes close, and I thump him on the forehead to get his attention again.

"Drugs are bad, Mannford. Surely you knew this with your mother being a doctor and all." I arch a brow at him. "How much oxy did you take?"

"Enough," Xavier assures me. "Fucker tried to

bite me, but he took his medicine like a good boy in the end."

"Harvard is gone," I bite out, thumping Scout again on the head. "Your weak attempt to coerce me into fixing your mistake was a waste of fucking breath. Your cars are gone thanks to your hot little sister. And now your mommy's ability to make money is gone too."

Scout's eyes widen despite the drugged haze he's in.

"She's being sued for malpractice." I shake my head as though I feel sorry for her. I don't. "By several people."

Perry chuckles. Ulrich, in his effort to uncover all he could about Manda Mannford, was able to find some people who were paid off for botched surgeries. All it took was a call from my attorney, the great Anthony Lambruski, offering to represent them for free and they quickly agreed their payoff wasn't enough for the terrible medical care they received.

"But wait, there's more," I say in a tone that mimics a gameshow host. "I have one more thing to take away from you." Rising to my feet, I stare down at the piece of shit triplets who thought they could go to war with me and win. They thought wrong. "Lacrosse."

I step back and gesture at Todd. He storms over to Sparrow, raises his foot, and stomps on his knee. Sparrow screams from behind the tape, tears streaming from his eyes. Sully whimpers when Todd makes his way over to him. Without warning, he does the same for Sully. Both sob like children. Finally, Todd delivers the same fate to Scout, making sure to smash both knees. Their howls of pain are music to my ears.

"Remember what I'm capable of," I spit out at Scout. "And this only scratches the surface of what I can do to you. I'm the king of this city, and you're nothing but bottom feeding parasites."

I give Xavier a nod of my head. He and Todd shove Sparrow and Sully into the backseat of their mother's Porsche. Then, Xavier comes back for Scout. He pushes him into the passenger seat and then closes the door before climbing in the driver's seat. Xavier gives me a mock salute before driving off. Todd hops into the SUV and follows him.

As soon as they're gone, Perry shakes his head and cringes. "Did you hear the pops? Fucking sick, man."

"Well deserved," I remind him. "Come on. We don't want to miss the show."

He follows me over to the lookout of the

parking garage that has a view of the street below. We wait patiently for several minutes. The white Porsche flies out onto the street, screeching as it turns sharply. It speeds up and then the door flings out, an ex-Navy Seal rolling out with impressive skill. The subsequent crash is loud.

Xavier hops to his feet, a knife in hand, making a beeline for the vehicle. He reaches in, cutting Scout's hands free and removing the tape on his mouth. Then, he drags him into the driver's seat. Todd pulls up in the SUV and quickly frees Sully and Sparrow. They close the doors and then hop into the SUV, disappearing down the next street. All of it happens within the course of a minute. Moments later, sirens can be heard as a police car makes it to the scene.

Their mommy will have a hard time cleaning up *that* mess.

CHAPTER TWENTY-TWO

ASH

Win: What are you doing?

Me: Waiting for you?

Win: Naked?

Me: I'm in a dressing room so…

Win: Want to make some money?

Me: Always.

Win: I'll be there soon. It'll be more fun in person.

"Everything okay in there?" the salesclerk asks, her voice bright and hopeful.

"Still trying things on."

I toss my phone back into my purse so I can pull on another dress. All the options the lady keeps bringing me are too fancy. I'd felt like an idiot walking in wearing cutoff shorts, a T-shirt, and flip flops. The woman who greeted me could barely fake a smile. However, when she realized I was here for the Constantine appointment, her smile got genuine real fast.

"Do you have anything…" I trail off with a

frown at my reflection. "Sexier?"

This dress looks like something an old lady would wear, not a woman about to go to dinner with a billionaire. It's sunshine yellow with embroidered daisies on it for God's sake.

"Mr. Constantine called ahead and asked me to locate our most demure dresses. I'm sorry if there was a miscommunication."

Ugh.

Winston did this on purpose.

Free embarrassment. I didn't even get paid for it. Fucker.

"No miscommunication," I grumble. "He's the one buying."

A deep chuckle resounds from the other side of the door. All my hairs stand on end in anticipation of seeing the face that goes with that voice. His rap on the door is sharp and demanding.

"Let me in, little girl."

"Daddy? Is that you?"

He snorts, waving his middle finger over the top of the door. "Open it, Cinderelliott."

With a stupid grin on my face, I unlock the door. He flings it open, his starved blue eyes devouring me in one hungry sweep over my body. With the way his nostrils flare, I'd say he's a fan of grandma dresses.

"Very conservative," he observes, a playful smirk tugging at his lips.

"Thinking about wearing it to our wedding."

He rolls his eyes. "Over my dead body."

"The wedding or the dress?"

I laugh when he ignores me, leaving the dressing room. A few minutes later, he returns with something I approve of. Short, fitted, black, sexy.

"Better." I take the dress from him and stand on my toes, waiting for a kiss. "Miss me?"

"Who are you again?"

"Your fiancée."

His blue eyes darken, but he makes no move to kiss me. I let out a huff. Before I can pull away, he clutches my throat, hauling me closer. Our lips meet for a hot kiss. The groan of need that escapes him does wonders for my ego. Maybe I *should* wear the granny dress. All too soon, he releases me. I hook the new dress on the hanger and then turn my back to Win so he can unzip me out of this yellow nightmare.

"Hmm." His grin is wolfish as he wraps his arms around my waist. "I thought you said you wanted to make some money."

I meet his wicked stare in the mirror. "Does it involve this horrible dress?"

"Let me fuck you in it."

Groaning, I try to pull away, but he doesn't let me go.

"You're not rich enough," I sass back at him.

At this, he laughs, rich and delicious. "Funny."

"I'm serious. You're going to have to get a loan to make that happen."

"Name your price, girlfriend."

"Not going to happen."

"Name. Your. Price."

"A bazillion dollars and a yacht."

"Bazillion isn't a real number."

"Fine, just a yacht."

"No." He slides his hands over my breasts, squeezing them. "How about three more years of college tuition dumped into your college fund?"

"To fuck me in this terrible dress?"

"And let me take pictures of course." He smirks. "Take it or leave it."

"Fine, but I get to wear the sexy dress to dinner."

"I'll allow it."

I roll my eyes. "And you have to call me baby while we fuck."

"You're obnoxious."

"You're just mad I've upped my negotiation

game."

"Mad? No. Impressed? Still no."

"Asshole."

"Bend over and let me see your ass, Cinderel-liott. I pay good money for it."

Flipping him off, I pull away and then bend over dramatically, wiggling my ass at him. His blue eyes dance with mirth before he smacks my butt. Then, he pushes up the stiff, yellow material to reveal my black panties. Slowly, he drags them down my thighs, letting them drop to my ankles.

"Aren't you afraid they'll hear?" I ask, my voice low and husky with need.

His fingers skitter along my ass crack and then tease my pussy. "I'm not afraid of anything," he murmurs. "Besides, they're taking a fifteen-minute break."

"Did you tell them we only need three?"

Smack!

I yelp and then scowl at him in the mirror.

"You're a mouthy one," he growls, dropping to his knees behind me. "Good thing I like your mouth."

And holy shit do I love his mouth. I whimper when his tongue laps at me from behind. He's not being shy or delicate. The man is messy and ravenous, licking and sucking and biting whatever flesh he can get to. He uses his hands to spread my cheeks apart in an obscene way that has me gasping. His tongue licks me in the most wicked place, and despite my skin turning red in the mirror, I love it. It's filthy and wrong, but boy does it feel right. Seeing this powerful billionaire on his knees behind me is addictive—a sight I'll never grow tired of seeing.

"Your asshole is adorable." He nips at my butt cheek. "*Baby.*"

"I hate you," I growl. "You always gotta ruin it."

His chuckle is hot and tickles my thighs. I moan when he pushes his tongue into my pussy, seemingly eager to taste every inch of me. My legs tremble and buckle the closer he brings me to orgasm. All it takes is a hard suck of my clit, and I'm seeing stars, begging for him to give me more.

"Hands on the mirror, *baby.*" He stands up and smacks my ass again. "Let me push your face against it while I fuck you, and I'll buy you your damn boat."

I nod because who doesn't want a yacht?

His fingers twist in my hair, and he yanks, turning my head so that my cheek rests on the cool surface. The sound of his belt coming undone and then the zipper going down makes me shiver. He manages to undress enough to pull his dick out and slaps it against my ass. I can't see my reflection—thank god for that since this dress is frightening to look at—but I imagine he's enjoying seeing me at his mercy. The groan that escapes him as he pushes into me with one thrust is empowering.

I drive this man crazy.

Me.

Not anyone else.

Just me.

"Unngh," I garble out, unable to form words or complete thoughts.

He barks out a harsh laugh, his thrusting hard and nearly painful. All I can do is hold on while he takes everything I have to offer. From this angle and at the forceful way with which he fucks into me, I lose all control with a yelp of his name. As I shudder with pleasure, he yanks out of me. Hot come splatters on my ass, claiming me as his.

"Oh no," he rumbles as he unzips my dress. "I guess I'll need to use this lovely dress to clean up the mess I made, *baby.*"

I hear the telltale sign of pictures being taken from his phone which causes a thrill to shoot through me. He then tugs the material down on the dress and uses it to swipe away his come.

Once he's satisfied, he strips it the rest of the way off me before pulling my panties back into place.

"You could go just like this," he offers, his large palms roaming up my bare ribs. "I wouldn't mind."

"You and half of New York." I reach over to grab the pretty black dress. "What should I name my yacht, fiancé?"

"Oh, for fuck's sake. You're going to name a boat too?"

"Naming boats is a thing," I argue. "How about 'Win's Sugar Baby'?"

"How about no."

I laugh as I slide on the dress. He zips me into it. His eyes narrow as he drinks in my appearance. Because I'm a brat, I spin around so he can admire the whole thing.

"Also a no," he growls, reaching for the zipper.

He knows I look good in this dress and the spoiled boy doesn't want anyone looking at what's his.

"Too bad." I smack his hand away. "I love it. I'm wearing this one."

He gives my ass a squeeze. "Hurry and find some shoes to go with it before I change my mind."

"Are you worried all the men we come across are going to try and steal your girlfriend away?" I taunt, grinning evilly at him.

"Not my girlfriend. And no."

"So sure?"

"Let us not forget about the last man who tried it."

I scowl at him. "What? What did you do?"

"Remember that twat at the bar who gave you his number?"

"Hot suited guy?"

His jaw clenches. "Wes. Unemployed now."

"You're evil, Winston Constantine."

"Tell me something I don't know, brat."

My mind reels as I find a pair of shoes and Winston pays the bill. Winston does a great job of pretending he doesn't care, but he does. He so does. It makes me want to sing it to him just to watch him deny it. I'm grinning by the time we make it to his car.

Not his car.

Perry's car.

"No," I groan. "Don't make me ride in it."

"You don't have a choice, Cinderelliott. Get in."

"Where's Perry?"

"He Ubered home."

"No." I gasp, glaring at him.

"No," he admits with a chuckle. "I wouldn't allow him in one of those disease-infested death traps. Mother circled back in her car to fetch him. I'll pick him up tomorrow."

I climb into the ugly orange muscle car and wait for him to join me. Once inside, he doesn't start the vehicle, just turns to look at me, intensity burning in his eyes.

"What?"

"I took care of it."

"Took care of what?"

"The triplets."

"Oh." I shiver at the mention of their name. "How?"

"Let's just say they got exactly what they deserve."

Before he can start the car, I climb over the console, straddling his lap. My fingers tease at the hairs at his nape as my mouth finds his. We kiss with an urgency we haven't had thus far in our bizarre relationship. I pour my gratefulness into the kiss. He returns it with vows to protect me no matter what. Neither of us have to speak, but I know.

He cares about me.

I'm more than an employee or a plaything.

I'm his.

"Win," I whisper against his lips. "I lo—"

"Don't." He nips at my bottom lip, silencing me. "You don't."

"I do."

"No, Cinderelliott, you don't. You're just infatuated. Thankful. But not that."

"I'm not a child." I glower at him.

"Your driver's license proves otherwise."

"I'm eighteen, dumbass."

"Eighteen. Still a teenager."

"A teenager your old ass is paying to fuck!"

"Exactly." He grabs my hips and all but tosses me back into my seat. "We have an agreement. You please me, and I pay you."

"Maybe I don't like those terms anymore."

"You don't get to renegotiate a better deal," he snaps back, rippling with anger. "Your college is paid for. I gave you a car. A fucking yacht. A whore apartment. Your bank account is loaded. I babysit your goddamn bird and employ you at my company. What more do you want from me?"

I swallow down the ball of emotion that now sits in my throat. "Everything."

"Greedy fucking girl."

He starts the loud engine, effectively ending the conversation. I buckle in and cross my arms over my chest, trying hard not to cry. I'm not crushing on him. It's more than that, and he knows it. I certainly don't feel things are one-sided either.

Winston Constantine is in denial.

One day he's going to have to face the facts.

He's falling for me and there's not a damn thing he can do about it.

CHAPTER TWENTY-THREE

WINSTON

S HE'S INSANE.

There's no way in hell she loves me. She can't. This is our game. Our fucking fun. Not love. Love can't exist in the Constantine world. That was proven at Dad's funeral. The love that does exist is more of a bond by last name—a loyalty to blood.

Ash forgets she's not the real Cinderella, and I'm most definitely not her Prince Charming.

She's a fucking maid.

I'm CEO of a billion-dollar company. Bored but so fucking rich I can pay for the kinkiest of services. All of which she gladly signs up for as long as the money comes through.

This is a transaction.

So why in the hell are you trying so hard to convince yourself, dumbass?

I ignore the argument in my head. As much as my stupid heart likes the idea of keeping Ash in my world as more than a sexy playmate, I can't. She's a liability. A goddamn risk. The Morellis already know she's something to me. It's why we can never be more.

My skin tingles with a mixture of fury and confusion. I'm mad that she would try and toss out those words so carelessly.

Love.

Ridiculous.

She's not in love with me. The girl has had all of one serious boyfriend. There's no way she could even begin to understand what real love is.

And you can, Constantine?

My only witness to love is my parents. Dad adored our mother. He spoiled her with gifts and attention and praise. Protected her at all costs. Defended her if anyone stood against her. Supported her in all her endeavors. He gave her everything she could possibly want or need and so much more.

We don't have that.

Liar.

I chance a glance at Ash. She's still fucking pouting with her arms crossed over her chest. Of course she looks good enough to eat in her tiny black dress. Whatever shampoo they used on her at the salon is to fucking die for. I crave to yank her back into my lap, bury my nose in her silky tresses, and inhale her scent. She's more addictive than those damn red gummy bears.

Her phone rings in her purse. She digs around and pulls it out to answer.

"Hey, Dad—"

Words are sucked out of her throat at whatever he says to her. Her palm goes to her mouth, covering it as though she's shocked at what he has to say. She nods even though he can't see her.

"Okay," she whispers. "Love you too."

As soon as she hangs up, she snaps her head my way. "Win, what did you do?"

"Regarding..."

"Don't be dumb." She smacks at my arm. "The triplets."

"I said I took care of it."

"You didn't explain," she huffs.

"They hurt you," I growl, sounding more like my father than I care to admit. "And they had to pay for that."

"I don't know how you managed this, but Dad said Scout was in big trouble for driving under the influence. All of them sustained similar injuries to their knees from the crash."

"They won't be playing lacrosse." I laugh, dark and cruel. "No Harvard. No lacrosse. No cars. No mommy to save them."

She winces. "You did something to Manda?"

"Manda did it to herself. All I did was expose it. She's going to have to answer for some surgeries gone wrong. It'll keep her busy and bleeding money while her sons sit in fucking jail for a bit."

"You did all this for me?"

I let out a derisive snort. "Don't read into it, Cinderelliott."

"Too late." Her voice takes on a teasing lilt that makes my dick very, very hard. "You can't deny it, Win. You loooooove me."

"Oh, fuck off, Ash."

She laughs and goddammit, I laugh too. After she digs around in her purse, she fishes out a bag from the candy store. As soon as she opens it and the car is filled with a familiar scent, I groan.

"Bought you a present, boyfriend."

"I'm through with those things."

"Liar. Open up."

Annoyed, but not really able to deny them, I part my lips. She pushes a gummy bear into my mouth, her fingers exploring, just begging to get trapped between my teeth. I bite down, giving her what she wants. When I'm sure I've left an indentation in her flesh, I release her fingers and suck as she pulls them away. The gummy bear remains on my tongue mixed with her unique taste.

"I bought Caroline some of these too since you love them so much." She puts one of the gummy bears in her mouth. I crave to stop at the next light, crash my lips to hers, and steal it right off her tongue.

"You bought my mother candy?"

"As a thank you. For the spa day."

"I'm pretty sure it was meant to be a threaten-the-maid-away-from-her-rich-boy day, but whatever, Ash. You see things for what they're not."

She waves her middle finger in front of my face, and I have the urge to bite it. "Sure, it may have started that way, but I grew on her. I have that way about me."

"No kidding," I gripe. "It's hard to get rid of you once you have your claws dug in."

Ignoring me, she continues. "Besides, I fig-ured her out."

"This should be good. Please. Do tell how you figured my mother out. We've only been trying our entire lives."

"Then it should be obvious to you." She feeds me another delicious-as-fuck gummy bear. "She is like one of those crazed bears in the forest. Scary and imposing. Hackles always raised and claws bared."

"I'm sure she'd love this comparison. Perhaps you should weave it into the conversation next time you see her."

"Because she's protecting her young," she continues with a sigh. "She's scary because she has to be. You Constantines may be terrifying bears—"

"Keaton says we're lions," I interject.

"Whatever. Big, scary beasts. Probably the highest on the food chain, yes?"

"Not probably. Most definitely."

"Your arrogance is suffocating me. Can we open a window?" she deadpans and then shakes her head as though annoyed. "But it doesn't mean you're not hunted, Win. Everyone is out to get you. Like the Morellis or that stupid Meredith."

Or whoever killed Dad.

I grit my teeth and nod. "So? They never succeed."

They did with Dad.

"Doesn't mean they won't ever. Regardless, because of this, Caroline has to always be ready to defend you all. To protect you at all costs."

"And how did this help you with my mother since you have it all figured out?"

"I did my best to impart to her that I'm not a threat to her children, especially you. That I'm an ally." She feeds me another gummy bear. "Team Constantine all the way."

"Hmm."

"Yeah, hmm."

"Don't get your hopes up," I tell her. "Mother may have been caught off guard by you." I certainly was. "But she'll regain her bearings and come back swinging. I hope you're ready to have your life flayed open."

"That happened the moment I sat on your desk and let you do filthy things to me," she sasses back. "I have nothing to hide." But the slight shift of her hazel eyes says otherwise.

My thoughts drift to earlier this evening after Perry and I dealt with the triplets. Nate texted me a warning, hinting that we had a mole within our ranks. He told me that if I'd ever get my head out of my ass and check her call log on her phone, maybe I'd realize this. At this point, his efforts to put a wedge between me and Ash rankles me. However, seeing the flicker of unease in Ash's gaze has me paying attention more closely, a seed of doubt planted and growing deep in my gut.

"For the record, I didn't do anything filthy that first day," I say, giving my head a slight shake to clear it. "Just spent some time up close and personal getting to know a little about my investment before I went all in."

"All in?" She grins at me. "I knew you were in love."

"Go to hell, Cinderelliott."

"Been there. Rode shotgun with your mean ass. Have the T-shirt."

I gun the engine, flying past several cars before turning into a parking garage. The engine echoes like a jet taking off inside the garage. There's an open space near the doors to the building where the restaurant is, and I whip into it. Once I park, I climb out, inhaling the lingering exhaust fumes from Perry's orange hotrod. Ash gets out of the car and straightens her short dress before pulling her purse strap over her shoulder.

Goddamn, she's beautiful.

The dress makes her long legs seem even longer. They're shiny tonight from whatever oils they put on her at the spa. My mouth waters to run my tongue up the inside of her thigh to taste her again.

We may not have love like she claims, but we have a damn good partnership going on right now. I know good business and sound investments. Ash was a risk, but it came with great reward. This thing between us is hot and entertaining. It's enough for me, so it has to be enough for her.

"Do you have reservations?" she asks when we reach the door and step inside the busy restaurant.

I place a palm on the small of her back. "I called ahead and spoke to the owner."

"Of course you did." She flashes me a silly smile that warms my blood.

"Have you been here before?" I ask, leaning in to inhale her sweet shampoo.

"No. Never."

"It's called Edge. A five-star steakhouse. The cows were probably still mooing this morning it's that fresh."

"Gross."

I laugh and shrug. "You won't say that once you've tasted the filet."

The hostess greets us. Once I murmur my name, her eyes widen, and she scurries off. Moments later, a portly man with a wiry beard greets us. He must be Ed Stevens, the owner.

"Mr. Constantine," he booms, shaking my hand. "So thrilled to have you at Edge tonight. Come this way."

He seats us at a table in the middle of the restaurant that faces the door. As requested. I give him a nod and guide Ash to her seat. Once I've pulled out the chair and seated her, I take my seat beside her.

"Look, he does know how to be a gentleman," she mutters to me, flashing me a wicked smile. "Who knew?"

I discreetly flip her off by scratching my stubble with my middle finger. "I want you to enjoy yourself tonight, Cinderelliott." It has cost me a *lot* of money.

She reaches over and squeezes my thigh under the table. "Even when you drive me insane, I have fun with you." She smirks. "*Boyfriend*."

Brat.

The restaurant is packed, but of course they found a way to indulge a Constantine. Money talks. In my case, it's super fucking chatty and anyone's willing to listen.

"Are you sure you've never been here before?" I cock my head to the side as I study her, lingering my stare on her plump lips.

"No. Not all of us are fancy like you," she teases.

"This is the Baldridge building. Where your stepmother works." Or *worked* if I have anything to say about it.

"No way," she hisses, her hazel eyes growing

wide and round. "This building is the one with the big fuss?"

I give her a clipped nod. "You never visited Manda?"

"No." Her nostrils flare in disgust. "I didn't."

The evening goes on without a hitch. Our appetizers are savory and delicious. Wine continues to flow. And the steak is every bit as I hyped it up to be. It's no wonder Leo Morelli wanted this building and plans to evict every tenant aside from Edge Steakhouse.

I'm watching Ash moan over chocolate cake when rats suddenly make their way into the building. Not actual rats. Morellis. Ash makes a choked sound upon seeing the entourage.

Oh good… dinner *and* a show.

CHAPTER TWENTY-FOUR

ASH

OH MY GOD.

He's here. That bastard is here.

Dread pools in the pit of my stomach, souring everything I just ate. With a shaking hand, I set the fork down with a clatter. I can't look at him, but I feel Leo's hard stare boring into me.

He wants to know Constantine secrets that I not only don't have, but I wouldn't give to him anyway. But the idea of him blasting our sex life to the world turns my stomach.

Dad will be disgusted.

Caroline will be horrified.

I tremble as I wonder how in the hell I'll get myself out of this mess. Winston doesn't know Leo's been harassing me. If he did…

What would he do?

One thing's for sure, he certainly wouldn't roll over and take it.

Against my own will, my eyes lift to track Leo.

He's seated at a table near the front door, his dark eyes locked on me. His attention falls to his phone, and then mine buzzes from inside my purse.

It's him.

I'm tempted to ignore him, but something tells me that won't bode well for me.

I scramble to grab my phone. The last thing I need or want is for Leo to come over here.

Asshole Stalker: *Why is Constantine in MY building?*

Great. Here we go.

Me: *He misses it.*

Asshole Stalker: *Don't fuck with me, sweetheart.*

Me: *I don't know why aside from the fact he likes the steak here!*

A picture comes through and it's one of the many explicit ones Winston has taken of me. My face burns with embarrassment and my gut twists almost painfully.

Me: *You're a pig.*

Asshole Stalker: *Just reminding you I hold all the cards. Again, why is Constantine in MY building?*

"They're all staring at us," Winston rumbles, his tone low and deadly. "The question is, why is Leo so fixated on you?"

I let out a helpless whimper, locking onto Winston's icy blue gaze. "I don't know."

Liar.

"I see." His eyes narrow and his jaw clenches. "Seems my mother and Nate know. It seems Leo fucking Morelli knows. Don't think for a second I believe that *you* don't know. Apparently, I'm the only damn idiot who *doesn't* know."

"Please, let's just leave." My whisper barely makes it over to him. Tears brim, and I make the mistake of glancing down at my phone. More filthy pictures.

"I want the truth. Who are you texting?"

The tears leak out, and I shoot Winston a devastated look. "Win…"

"Answer one question. Yes or no." The air crackles with tension as Winston peels me apart layer by layer with just one look. He's always been good at getting inside my head. With Winston, I don't know that I ever had a chance to keep him out. "Is Leo Morelli texting you?"

"Win, please."

"Answer the goddamn question."

I swipe away the tears on one cheek with the

palm of my hand. Glancing down, I find several text threats and more pictures. Leo is assuming I told Winston which means I've broken my end of the agreement. He's going to send these pictures and videos to every news outlet and television station.

I'm going to be sick.

"I'm so sorry," I choke out. "I can explain."

"How long have you kept this from me?" he demands, his voice barely audible. "How long have you been talking to that rat behind my back about who the fuck knows what?"

I sniffle as I admit the inevitable, "Since your birthday party."

His icy blue eyes harden as the betrayal of what I've done becomes clear in his mind.

He's no Prince Charming.

He's the king of everything.

A master manipulator. A puppeteer pulling all the strings. A designer of a tricky game.

Wicked. Ruthless. A bit crazy.

And I've wronged him in the worst possible way.

Thank you for reading PRINCE CHARMING! Don't miss the stunning conclusion of the Cinderella trilogy! You can order THE GLASS SLIPPER right now…

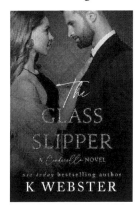

Betraying the most powerful man in New York wasn't something I ever envisioned when I first started playing games with Winston Constantine. But he's engaged in far more dangerous games than ours, and his enemies are out for blood.

Winston has my heart, the Morellis have incriminating photos, and I'm left with nothing except three stepbrothers who want to hurt me and a future in doubt. I knew Winston wouldn't be my prince charming, but that didn't stop me from falling for him.

After all, the slippers fit, and I let myself believe I'd be dancing with Winston forever.

Until too much truth comes to light.

Until I realize instead of ruling the board, I was just a pawn.

In the end, I have only one question. When his game with me is over, will I be able to pretend as if the glass slipper wasn't a perfect fit?

The warring Morelli and Constantine families have enough bad blood to fill an ocean, and their brand-new stories will be told by your favorite dangerous romance authors. See what books are available now and sign up to get notified about new releases here…

www.dangerouspress.com

About Midnight Dynasty

Midnight Dynasty is a world where enemies and lovers are often one and the same.

JOIN THE FACEBOOK GROUP HERE
www.dangerouspress.com/facebook

FOLLOW US ON INSTAGRAM
www.instagram.com/dangerouspress

SIGN UP FOR THE NEWSLETTER
www.dangerouspress.com

Copyright

Printed in Great Britain
by Amazon